Stories from the Mandel House

Also by Hermann Stehr from K A Nitz:

The Engraver

Meicke, the Devil

The Shingle Maker and Other Tales

Leonore Griebel

The Buried God

The Shimmer of the Assistant and Other Tales

The Twilight and Other Tales

Three Nights

Stories from the Mandel House

Hermann Stehr

K A Nitz

WELLINGTON

*For Mrs Margarete Hauptmann,
in thanks for many a dream
her violin has sung to me.*

1

All women grow and decay in the position which they sprout from, like flowers, and even if they were led by their star halfway around the world.

Men, however, are always chased across the entire earth by their unease and find their feet again only a little when the shadow of the church tower reaches out into the field. This current of unrest is like a wind which holds their soul constantly in breath. Sometimes it is colourful, sometimes hot, sometimes dry, according to age.

Eusebius Mandel, the tailor of Upper Röhrsdorf, had already stepped into the raw, stiff wind. When it blew against men, they stood with their life already before the Virgin's birth.

Most of the swallows had gone, here and there cobwebs already nestled on the stubble, and they had to bend their backs to make progress. So it was around the Röhrsdorf tailor. The path he was walking whirred sometimes in front of his eyes like a tautened cord someone was marking, and he had to squint so that he did not stray left or right to somewhere he had nothing to seek. This precise gaze had already written all kinds of scratches on his temples, and his hair was curling white over his ears.

Sometimes he stood on the slope behind his house and observed the world: the farmers ploughing across the field; the wood carters next to their high wheeled carts or the baker whirring past in his little wagon. And when he had thus looked down on the world for a while, he took his handkerchief out, spread it out as if he wanted to wrap it around something, but then folded it up again and shoved it in his coat. For it seemed obvious, Eusebius Mandel could not deny that the others made progress easier and more happily than he did.

And since he possessed a nimble spirit, why it was so did not remain hidden to him either. They had children. That is for men, however, no different than if holy grass grew between the dusty grey stones of their path, and no different than if the spring broke forth from heavy autumn clouds unexpectedly and incomprehensibly, and the stiff wind of age had no genuine power over such men.

And Eusebius Mandel blossomed every time into a great yearning after he had looked down from the slope over life. The entire tailor then became a tightly drawn thread and also like a nail which sticks out to jab you. But before he got home, he had already lost his industrious bearing, and there was nothing doing again about the child, not even about a girl which the Lord would merely shake out of her clothes.

Only Eusebius would not have been called Mandel, who had seen more than a hundred eyes could bear and fifteen hands could grasp, if he had slept on his hopes. Once he stuck to the correct path and, three days later, his wife, Agathe, looked at him, blushed and said, "Eusebius, I think, this time I really am with child."

She remained so too; and because long expectations have no other sense than to enrich their fulfilment, if you consider it rightly, it lay entirely in the cut, as Eusebius would say, that the little one Agathe bore was a little boy. Not only that. The little Mandel's birthday even lay on a Sunday near the summer solstice. His father, who was actually called Christoph as well, took that as a good sign, and because the midwife had looked in the almanac and found that the boy's hour of appearance, the first hour after midnight, already fell under the influence of Gemini, his father was doubly happy.

The little Mandel had barely been contemplated in the trembling circle of light from the tallow candle when the clever woman made two large crosses over his eyes, his head, his hands and his lap, so that he would truly have doubled everything desirable. Christoph nodded at everything. Only when the midwife outlined the cross over his lap, he coughed into his hand and left the room.

In the morning, after a short sleep, he had mastered this misgiving and strode in a confident mood around his little house. Every four steps, he said to himself, "Double the honour", or "double the money", or "double the cleverness". Only when he said, "double the number of children", he stood still and looked through the large maple into the heavens and thought, 'He up there will already know what is appropriate.' Thus Christoph Eusebius Mandel built castles in the air amongst the clouds for his son.

The midwife left that afternoon. Mandel sat on his wife's bed and told her of the great fortune her son would enjoy because he had come into the world under Gemini.

Only his wife just shook her head weakly, for she could not speak well yet and what she had to say was too much. But her husband got all the more agitated because he thought she would have preferred a girl and begrudged him the boy. In the end, he swore to call him Amadeus and not deviate from it even if the Pastor set heaven and hell in motion against it.

But the more Mandel got worked up, the paler his Agathe became. For that reason, he suddenly bit off the smouldering threads and contented himself with walking back and forth in the room and striking harder with his heel every fourth step, at which he comprehended his own thoughts. Thus he proved himself right and Agathe received her rest.

She turned her bloodless face to the wall and cried silently to herself, because she thought that what had been foretold beyond all measure could not prosper. Then she felt with her hand next to herself and moved the little one closer to herself to ask him for forgiveness if God had destined him for something great.

Towards evening an incomprehensible fear came over her. But she swallowed her sorrow until, towards midnight, it could not be endured anymore. Then she called her husband's name softly. He climbed out of bed on the third call, lit a candle and came to her.

"Christoph," she said, "am I not forty?"

"Yes."

"Haven't we waited a long time for a child?"

"And now we have one."

"Why should our boy's life be wound up and bound already on his first day?"

Christoph was already out of his intoxication of joy and agreed with his wife over everything. He asked her not to excite herself, covered her up carefully, extinguished the light and toddled back to his bed.

But the new mother was so weak she could not get away from the thought that her husband's exuberance had brought misfortune onto the child. The fright overwhelmed her so that a cold sweat broke forth from her body's pores. She could not open her mouth, for it was as if someone had pressed a large hand over it.

At dawn she saw three women in grey vestments. They were being driven here and there by the wind so that they were always gliding past the window. The haunting image would not stop. So she collected all her strength and turned towards the wall so as not to suck the unfriendly spirits into her room with her glance. She tried to pray. Only the words became like a swirling fire circling before her closed eyes. After a few vain endeavours, she turned to the room again to ascertain whether the grey spirits had been driven away. But just then, she saw the last one waft into the room and place itself by the other two on her bed. Then the new mother lay still and felt hot air skimming over her. It was sinking deeper and deeper into her. When it had arrived at her heart, the blood released itself from the chambers and ran out from them.

Not long afterwards, Christoph awoke and approached her bed to tell her about the beautiful dreams which had played out before his bed towards morning. But his wife could not answer and the look of her large, blue eyes had turned rigidly to where no love and no human power could avert them anymore.

He saw that she had died. Only, no man is capable of facing up so easily to that gruesome wonder which is death and while poor Christoph's tears flowed from his eyes and words of prayer from his lips, he grasped with his hand and sought whether in her heart, that deepest firepit of life, a poor little spark still burnt which, tended with devotion, could be reestablished. Only death had also settled down there, and the filled breast lay like a hard, cold stone on it. Then Mandel thought with fright of what would now become of his little Amadeus.

He sprang up and, as he was, one suspender over his shoulder, the other still hanging down behind, ran down the street to fetch the midwife. The suspender, on which his wife had embroidered a burning heart with red wool, flapped constantly against his leg as he ran. Whenever he was thus in danger of falling, he leapt, and every time it was about to bring him to the ground, he said, "Fall down, tailor, and die!"

But every time, he thought of his little Amadeus and his cold wife, who perhaps was not yet dead, and took back his imprecation. In this way, it did not take long before he was at the midwife's place. She stood on the lawn before her door and was striking the dust from her Sunday frock with a hazel switch as it hung from the lowest branch of a plum tree. When she had heard from Christoph Eusebius what it was all about, she laid the hazel switch aslant in the tree, ducked, let the frock glide over her from above and bound it fast on the way. While she advanced hastily, she asked the tailor this and that, how the misfortune had happened so fast and many other things. But he stared down in front of himself and counted the stones on the path in grief. When she poked him, he turned his hollow face to her and smiled agonisingly. Then she fell silent at last, until they arrived at the tailor's house, whose door stood wide open. Beneath the narrow wooden bench lay a bundle and a stick. The midwife wanted to know who had tended the house for Mandel while he was away. But Christoph did not answer, for he thought it was the burden and stick of death, who wandered restlessly over the earth, and that when they arrived at the dead one, they would see him already next to the chair by the bed, in the pose of a man who had finished a work and, between staying and going, was looking over the completed work once more with sober eyes.

They arrived in the room which was quiet with the stagnant breath of the dead woman and yet also peaceful in the morning light which was throwing a green shimmer through the maple's crown. And really, when Christoph, who had closed the door behind the midwife, turned around, he saw a dark figure draw back soundlessly from the bed of the dead woman into the depths of the room and crouch down there while it inclined its lowered head even more. Christoph was in such a despairing mood that even this terrible confirmation of his thoughts hardly touched him, and he stepped with the midwife to the bed of the woman who had passed away. There he now recognised sure enough from her blue lips that there was no more hope.

"Did she die from her soul, that is from the centre of her being, or from her body?" he asked so quietly that he was barely heard, for he was reproaching himself for having driven his wife to her death through his stubborn, loud hopes.

But the midwife grasped his gaunt, cool tailor's hand with her fat, warm right hand and answered, "Her life blood is gone. Who takes it away, I don't know, that only God knows."

With that she reached over, pressed the dead woman's eyes shut and wished her a happy journey to heaven and a good reception with the Father.

It all seized the tailor Mandel so much that he forgot death in the corner, his little Amadeus and everything in the world. He sank down on the bed and cried into the stiff hand of his wife who had endured all the grief and love with him for so many years. It lasted a very long time, for the smaller and poorer a man is, the greater is his pain. The pressure of a hand on his shoulder tore him from the circles of his hardship. He was shocked to the tips of his hair for a moment, for he thought death had touched him too and wanted to take him as well. When he dared to turn around, the figure which he had taken for death had vanished from the corner and a full, fresh woman was standing next to the midwife, making a painfully friendly face and cradling the small bundle, his Amadeus, maternally in her arms. Then his glance unwrapped itself completely from the entanglements and he recognised in the youthful woman the deaf-mute

Maruschka from Bohemia, who had always undertaken a journey for weeks into Prussia, because they did not take care of the poor so well up there. Every time she wandered home again with full load, she had stayed a night under the tailor's small roof. Now she found her kind hostess among the dead. The soul of man is not Prussian and not Bohemian; in its best hours, it talks like a god in the language of all men.

Although nothing went in poor Maruschka's ears and nothing came out her mouth, she understood the tailor quite easily: if the King of Prussia allowed it and the tailor Mandel had nothing against it, she wanted to stay with him until he had found a better nurse, take care of the little child and lead his household including the garden and the two white goats.

On the morning of the third day, the bells of the local church at Neudorf called out over the expanse of tree-tops of the Hainwald forest to the tailor's house, and the graveyard demanded the dead woman. The children's dirge swelled and sank into the blue air. The wooden wagon with the black coffin covered in green fir branches went away. Just the one time, the tailor's wife travelled in a wagon to church, and this time she never returned.

The maple tree moved its branches and a ripple ran through its crown.

Little Amadeus lay awake on his pillow, and it seemed like he was listening to the sound in the air.

2

When, on the seventh Sunday, Christoph had furtively placed the bunch of fresh flowers on his wife's grave again, he did not quarrel so bitterly anymore with the fate which had carried her away from him, and he began humbly to not begrudge the Lord.

Until then he had left the brown and black striped, half-woolen skirt and the blue-flowered jacket, which Agathe had worn on the last Sunday of her life, hanging on the coat hooks next to her bed so as to not do without the comforting illusion that his dear wife could any moment step over the threshold and go through the house as busily as usual, as if death had been nothing but a long walk to church. Now he laid her things in a chest, covered them in newspaper to protect against moths, nailed the lid shut with long nails and placed the chest on the floor in a corner.

This reconciliation with the pain slowly blotted out the deathly face with which the dead woman looked up at him from his soul, and more and more he saw her in everything on which her eyes had rested in life. She looked into his room with the light emerging from behind the mountains; the little stream below the meadow had her voice; the flowers looked at him with her eyes. She hummed in the rustling of the maple into his dreams.

His thread found the eye again by itself like in the good days. The needle skipped up and down animatedly, and if the sorrow crept up on him again, he pierced it all over and strangled its vapour with the threads. When he was free of such visitations, he spun out the hopes which had been so abruptly torn away. For the Pastor had not denied his boy the beautiful, opulent name Amadeus, but just smiled kindly over it. It was thus as if the child had now opened the door wide into the wide, opulent world, and when it had grown tall, it would be permitted to go and gather it up with its two healthy arms to its heart's content. Sometimes he was completely enraptured over the fortune his Amadeus would one day be able to enjoy. He threw his work on his cutting table, took the little one in his arms, showed him the sun, the flowers, the sky and said, "Your mother is up there."

Thus Christoph Eusebius's life divided itself between his work and his child. But he liked most of all to be with him and forgot that there was a tavern in which to sit, and men with whom you could chat for pleasure. When Maruschka carried the boy into the garden in front of his windows, he also shared in their joy. Since the poor foster mother's mouth was blocked off, little Amadeus was not captured so early by the words of men and blossomed and absorbed himself deep in the thousand songs which God himself plays with the trees, the birds, the water and the wind. Soon it was possible to have him ride on the goats while someone supported his shoulders. He sprang out of the little smock and into his first trousers. Then he was a real boy, strolling about with a stick in the garden and blowing through the hollow stems of the mayflowers.

Many times, and they remained the most beautiful of his life, fortunately and sorrowfully too, little Amadeus sat next to his father at the cutting table. When he lifted him up, he pressed a kiss every time on his blond parting, and his glance probably then looked for a while animatedly through the crack in the present at what had once been. Only Eusebius did not dive into the shadows for long. For such a tailor gets something in his spirit from the needle which he plies, something sharply decisive, which admittedly flips with many into a comical vanity. And as the pointed, shiny, little steel lance stitched together an orderly measured dress quickly and certainly from a confused heap of patches, the tailor succeeded above all in turning the colourful accidents of his life into a well-ordered world and spreading it out around him. It worked out still better for Christoph Eusebius, and that only because he was actually, to say it with due respect, only a mender of clothes. For this reason, he never submerged his senses completely in his work. With the best of his spirit, while he stitched away with crossed legs, he twisted and turned his life about until it had been turned into a quite orderly career, which doubtleesly allowed him to rejoice over it.

Then he sometimes told Amadeus about it. He enjoyed it most of all when he came to speak of his Hildesheim trip. This in particular formed the high point of his life.

Thus he said, "The capital of the world is in Berlin. There are so many people there that they don't have room on God's earth and that's why thousands journey constantly over the rooves; others travel for pure enjoyment into deep holes and come out safe and sound again on the other side. The Emperor lives there too, when he is at home with the Empress. Increasingly, however, he goes out in his coach and can make the world stand still. Now I did not see him, and because they were making trousers far too wide in Berlin at the time, I did not enjoy myself for long and so I tied up my rucksack to go see France. I walked and walked. Finally such a city stood before me again, and the bells sounded so loudly from the towers that you'd think all the people were hanging on the bell ropes and pulling with all their strength. When I asked a woman, who was running as hastily as if she were making off from the noise, what the good city with the loud bells was called, she said, 'Hildesheim', and continued running. Aha, I thought,

Hildesheim, a fine name! And I went in and asked about work. Received it too in a beautiful house with a master who had a beard like Napoleon. But that went against the grain with me for a moment, for the beard was slanted like a saw and long like a chisel, like that which always grows on the devil's side. Was even so. For hardly had I sat down than I broke three needles. In this way, I had my day's work brought to an end straight-away, for Napoleon didn't think he needed a journeyman for breaking needles, the apprentices were there for that. I was quite content with that. With a tailor who doesn't have enough needles in his drawer, the bailiff must already be standing behind the door. That can be tolerated by whoever wants it, I said, and found myself in an instant on the street. Then I had what I wanted; I also found myself not long afterwards on the road that led to Paris. As I walked along and counted the stones which stood by the gutter, and thought of how many thousand must run past me before I would see the first red trousers, it came up behind me: trapp, trapp, and again, trapp, trapp. I turned around. A solitary horse was approaching. No man to be seen far and wide, and the reins were dragging on the road. I let it go a little past me, then ran after it and grasped the reins. Then the horse thought the wagon was behind it and stopped. It was a bay and so well fed that the hollows were gone from its cheeks. Now when I slapped it, it looked at me and blinked with its eyes as if it had already known me a long time. That's why I bound the reins up, led it to a stone and swung myself onto its back. Ask in the next village who it belongs to, I thought. For I knew well that the Lord does not from one moment to the next gift a handworker like me a spotless bay. If it belonged to nobody, then I would ride to France like Blücher. Meanwhile I would let my steed feel the stick. Then it threw the earth away under itself like gingerbread, and the trees next to me cowered so primly when I flashed by. That went on until evening, and I felt neither hunger nor thirst, for when I looked left and right over the fields which were turning slowly like a millstone, it seemed no different than if everything belonged to me.

Finally I saw the first star appear over the peak of my cap. Houses and farms leapt up and down before me, and people stood at their doors and opened their eyes wide in surprise. I pulled my horse by the halter so that there were sparks and before I could correct myself, I had come off. When everything was back in order, I asked politely about the owner of my fearless travelling companion. Not long after, a man stood before me who seemed knocked together out of planks and beams and looked me steadily in the face. When he observed that I was just as good and stalwart a fellow, he grinned and offered me his large, fat hand with many thank yous and said the bay belonged to him. In my hand, however, he left behind a hard, shiny Mansfeld taler. I was delighted with the trade, for an honest taler is better than a stolen horse."

"Did you arrive in France then?" Amadeus asked, when Eusebius broke off at this point. But the tailor then said neither yes nor no, but continued, "It was similar in Cologne, or it amounted to the same, as running into a butcher's yard halfway to Hamburg." So it remained indecisive as to whether Christoph Eusebius had ever seen Hamburg. But for little Amadeus, the name slowly became like a large, illuminated gate behind which every wonder existed, and his father, who would soon have been there, seemed stranger to him than any man. The tailor thus passed over this fact, which so excited his little son, with the strict matter-of-factness of a widely travelled man and soon started on a new adventure, and while the golden mountains of France still lay before the little boy's eyes, he probably noticed that his father's needle had already journeyed on again in thought. For whether Christoph Eusebius told of the cathedral in Cologne, the salt works in Halle, the wide ocean or a forest which had no end, he plied his needle accordingly. He sewed all his wanderings into the clothes people brought to him. Now sometimes that did not redound to his advantage at all. For when he had sewed into the back of a farmer's trousers the large level square before the royal palace in Berlin, it sure enough did not want to concede to the excessive rounding which grew there from a real farmer. And when the man of the land nevertheless carried through his will and, spreading his legs, fell on his knees, the King of Prussia just had to yield and let his beautiful square go to smithereens. It did not turn out much better with other adventures which the tailor Mandel incorporated into other people's things, and his reputation fell rather than rose. But there were still always enough people who rewarded him with work. His needle speared pfennig after pfennig from the pockets of customers, earned beam after beam of his house, carried him simply through life and gave him abundant opportunity to fill his son's soul with colourful, strange stories and dreams.

3

Amadeus lived in amazing stories longer than other children. But even with him, morning and evening coalesced into the first day and he awoke to the life of the others.

As always, he sat with his little pot of milk and his slice of bread, his breakfast, on the footstool in front of the chair and looked out the window. Everything which had been dreamily familiar now appeared mysterious to him.

The willow in the meadow, which he had often looked at, was slouching there as if looking at its feet.

"Why is the tree standing in the meadow?" he asked his father.

"Because they planted it there."

"Why did they plant it there?"

"Because of the shade."

"What is that: shade?"

"It is black and cool and lies under the tree."

"Who does the shade belong to?"

"To the tree, Amadeus."

Then the little boy took a bite of his bread and a swallow of his milk. He turned around and looked at his neighbour's red tiled roof.

"Who does the red roof belong to?"

"To the farmer Schnallke."

"Why isn't he a tailor?"

"Because he has cows and horses."

"Why does he live next to us, and we have no cows or horses?"

"He belongs to the village, boy."

"Is the village also called Schnallke?"

"No, it's called Röhrsdorf, lies in the county Mittelschwer and belongs to the Kingdom of Prussia."

After a while, Amadeus bent down and looked through the little window at the heavens to see how high the Kingdom of Prussia went.

"Does the King of Prussia live there?"

Christoph Eusebius climbed from his cutting table, bent down also and looked along the arm of the little boy.

"No, Amadeus, that isn't a house, that is the long bush."

"But the King lives behind it."

"No, there your aunt lives, and when you are big and diligent at school, we will go through the bush to her."

Eusebius returned to his cutting table and grinned over Amadeus being such a bright-eyed boy. The little boy finished his breakfast thoughtfully. Then he again looked attentively and thoroughly out each window. Finally he shook his little head and asked apprehensively, "Does the village of Röhrsdorf belong to us?"

"Certainly, Amadeus," old Mandel answered, "for we live there."

This information dislodged the chagrin from the little boy's face, and he left the room brightened.

Outside, not very far from the house, he climbed onto a heap of field stones to investigate how big his father's village was. Every time he saw a house, he said, "Röhrsdorf", and the more rooves appeared before his astonished eyes, the happier he became, and finally he sang the name of his hometown, about his father, and wove a song about the King of Prussia as well. What he sang, stormed quite ungovernably as long as it was near him, but as soon as it had flown deeper into the bright air, it became more brilliant, more alien to him. And nothing was capable of checking his song. It glided over the stalks of grass so that they trembled, it touched the trees so that they became greener, and it reached right up to the red sun and seemed up there to detach deep, peaceful sounds from the wheel of fire onto the blue sheet. Sometimes it seemed as if these sounds were sinking down straight from heaven, then it seemed to him again as if they were being carried over the Hainwald forest. Now he perceived clearly that it was the bells of Neudeck, and fell silent, dismayed because he thought his voice had emitted them and that they had to sound so long as he was singing. They indeed fell silent after a while and Amadeus thought that if he were the King of Prussia then his singing would have such power that it would awake the church bells all over the world. On the road below, a wagon occasionally travelled to Berlin or Hildesheim. And Amadeus realised that if he wanted to become a king who commanded the whole world with his voice, he must first have a city. That's why he climbed down from the heap of stones and erected a wall from large stones, behind which he constructed Hildesheim. Tall, thin stones were the towers; long, oblong chunks formed the houses. There were also little houses, twee little nodes which made Amadeus laugh that people could be so stupid as to live in them. When he found a discarded matchbox on the path, he was not short of people and bells anymore. He broke the box's drawer up and had four people: two big and two small. One of the long slivers was a woman running from the city because it rang too loud with bells there.

She stood bent over next to the wall. So that she was able to get out, he took a stone out of the wall and now had the most beautiful gate. The little slivers, the women's children who wanted to flee with their mother, had fallen and lay pathetically in front of the city from whose tallest tower wobbled the bell, the sleeve on a crosswise matchstick. Amadeus did not begrudge them any peace. He continually prodded it with his finger and tolled with his voice at the same time, even if the woman was quite distressed and her poor children were lying on their faces. Only, now his father would enter Hildesheim, and yet no bridge has been built over the old gutter so he could cross the great river. Amadeus held the travelling Eusebius, the other long sliver, in his hand and did not know for a moment how to help. As he looked out over all sides of the meadow and thought someone must come from Berlin or Hamburg, a call came from the farmer Schnallke's shed, "Smithie, here!" and soon, behind a pomeranian dog dancing in the grass and comically flapping now the one, now the other long ear, the farmer's little boy appeared. When he spotted Amadeus, he shouted even louder at his dog. Little Mandel, who was standing next to Hildesheim and had stuck his father among the stones, wished that Smithie, the pomeranian, would come over so that he could stroke it. But he did not stir, and even when the dog was by him and sniffing at his leg, he did not grasp him because of an uneasy feeling which he was receiving from the Schnallke boy. He was a solid little fellow with a button nose and a bold, healthy face. His brown hair was all matted like the bristles of a collapsed butter brush used for greasing cake tins and one of his leather trouser legs was without ties below.

When he came near, he grasped the dog by the long hair of its neck and asked, "Are you perhaps the tailor's boy?"

Amadeus did not answer, sat down next to the town wall and covered up his father with his hand warily. This taciturnity obviously annoyed the little farmer, and to prove what sort of man he was, he said, "The meadow belongs to us. There is our farm, and there is our corn."

"And the willow?" Amadeus asked.

"It belongs to us too."

Little Mandel laughed; for he knew better. Then the Schnallke boy got excited and shouted, "The tree and that and that behind it, and the others and the whole bush, all of it, all of it belongs to us, and I am Martin Schnallke."

He ran around the heap of stones and pointed at the whole world. When he tried to walk past, Amadeus grasped at his trousers to find out what sort of material they were.

Actually Martin wanted to run home to complain to his father that sitting outside in the front meadow was a boy who did not believe everything belonged to the farmer Schnallke. But when he felt the little tailor's hand on his leg and noticed a puzzled expression on his face, he calmed down and said importantly, "Yes, yes. They are leather trousers. Do you perhaps think they aren't mine?"

Amadeus closed his hand more firmly over his father, and asked, "Who does the village belong to?"

"Our village?"

"Well, Röhrsdorf?"

"Perhaps not to you?"

Now little Mandel's great moment had arrived. He rose and said with deep earnesty, "It belongs to the King of Prussia."

Then Martin Schnallke was very frightened and sat down next to Amadeus, and he told him about the Kingdom of Prussian. It went up to the heavens and behind the forest, and the King of Prussia lived still much further away than his aunt, had trousers as wide as corn sacks and did not need to be at home at all like other men but travelled constantly on all the railways.

Then they played "Hildesheim". Martin Schnallke became the bell ringer of Hildesheim and rejoiced that the woman ran away and the children lay there and screamed. He wiggled the matchbox without break and tolled with his voice as loud as he could so as to scare the poor children to their deaths. But Amadeus led his father amidst much danger through the unending grass forest to Hildesheim and had him hold a quite well-mannered conversation with the woman at the gate.

The pomeranian Smithie, however, lay in the moat around the city and slept. When the bells tolled far too loud, he straightened up a little, held his head half inclined and lifted an ear.

The Hildesheim game would have gone on beautifully the whole day long if Martin had not also wanted to command the journeyman. But Amadeus could not allow that because it was his father. He did not say anything about that though, but placed himself in front of the gutter and safeguarded Eusebius, who was just then stuck deep in the grass forest on his march to Berlin.

After some back and forth, Martin finally lost patience, knocked over all of Hildesheim, sought out the journeyman and stamped him into the earth with curses. When Amadeus saw his father played with so wickedly, he plunged, crying for help, at the Schnallke boy. But he pushed little Mandel away once more and then began trotting across the meadow because the door to the tailor's house had creaked open.

He had just reached the corner of the shed when Eusebius appeared in the yard. He probably noticed straightaway who the guilty one had been in the affair. But instead of going to get a hold on the little terror, he went over to his boy who was lying on the ground and digging a little sliver from the ground with sobs. To all the questions over what Martin had done to him, he just cried constantly in distress, "He trampled him." So Eusebius lifted him up and lead him into the house. But before he vanished behind the door, his calm broke and he launched a heathen-like hail of curses and threats at Martin's head which came out from time to time from behind the corner of the shed. But when he laid off once to catch his breath, the Schnallke boy shouted from his hiding place, "Tale-teller! Bitpiece tailor!"

Then Eusebius thought it best to clear the field so that his son would not have to hear these disrespectful words anymore; for whoever presses too long with a hot iron in one place will incinerate the best fabric.

Inside, Maruschka received the vanquished boy, cleaned the dirt from his trousers and comforted him with affectionate, gurgled sounds. She spurred Eusebius on to revenge with fist gestures. He looked for a while at her excited face, at her heaving breasts and blinked, as was his fashion when something odd occurred to him. Then he stepped up to her and pressed her arms down against her body. That would mean: go and do your work!

And that the tailor did, although he was still protesting inwardly. But it seemed impossible for him to see these bare, plump arms in front of him, for then he would have to rush out and scream anew, and it was no better when his hands were touching the woman's soft, hot flesh. No, something like the instinct to flee seized him for a moment. For that reason, he let go of the mute and went to his cutting table, shaking his head. There he sewed the entire story into the sleeve which he had before him, his fury in the meadow and his trembling in the house. His needle described long, abrupt thrusts and his face was red like the time he had talked of Napoleon's work. The light in the room swayed as though drunk and the air in it was so thick it barely passed through Mandel's lungs. When Maruschka left the room to work in the garden, the rings of the sun stopped dancing across the floor and everything had its measured appearance again. The tailor straightened up from his work and looked around for his boy. He was leaning in a corner next to the pot cupboard. His face was pale and frightened, and his sight lay painfully on his father as if something terrible had just happened which he could not comprehend. Mandel laid the jacket down and led the intimidated boy to the chair. Whilst doing this, he talked affectionately to him. He forbade him from playing with Martin again as he had the devil in his body and was the offspring of a father who kept two wives. And if he promised him never to stroll about without permission, then he would buy him a slate and a pen so that he could write and draw whatever occurred to him.

Little Amadeus sat next to the chair on the little footstool and listened to everything his father said. But when his father was sitting at his cutting table again and gently plying his needle, the tears began to flow from the boy's eyes again quite silently. For he was sad that the Schnallke boy had two mothers and he had just one who could neither speak nor sing. At the same time, it was a recognised devil's boy who had knocked over Hildesheim and trampled on his father. And when he came to this point and looked at his father covertly from the side, it did not appear quite so certain to Amadeus anymore that Röhrsdorf belonged to him.

His world had received a kick. A slipping and changing came over everything in his soul. It was sometimes so strong that he did not dare to stand up when he was sitting, and did not have the courage to stand still when he was running. He had arrived in none other than a foreign place and yet his father's house stood around him as ever.

At supper he suddenly looked up from his plate and directed his pale blue, calm eyes at the mute Maruschka for a long time.

Then he asked his father, "Why can't Maruschka-mother talk and I can?"

"Your mother is in heaven", Eusebius answered and turned his face away at the same time so that his house-keeper could not read his lips.

"Isn't Maruschka-mother my mother?" Amadeus asked further.

"Oh yes, she is yours too."

With that little Mandel was immensely delighted.

"Then I also have two mothers like Martin", he cried, "and you also have two wives like the farmer Schnallke."

Eusebius gave no answer to this, stepped to the window and wiped his face with his handkerchief. On his return, he was still blinking and said a midge had flown into his eye. Maruschka, who had also understood his words, wanted to wipe the little creature out and was already stretching out her hand to him. But for the world, the tailor could not have endured her handling him now. He shook his head, went out and leaned over the fence. The sky was already deep blue from the approaching night and behind the forest of the long bush, a white glow was climbing up. The tailor Mandel's thoughts tailed off into it.

Maruschka waited a while for Mandel to return and finish his supper. But when he was too long in coming, she went out too and presented herself to him. Amadeus remained alone in the room, for he was all too happy that he now also had two mothers like Martin Schnallke. And he thought sometimes of the one and sometimes of the other. When he closed his eyes and contemplated the mute then the twilight in the room became even greyer and the walls began to emanate a deep, monotonous humming. But when he steered his dreams to his other mother, who according to his father's words lived in heaven, then everything was immersed in a white light and he heard ringing and singing quite far off. For that reason, he wished the two would swap places with each other so that his heavenly mother could be with him again, cook him good food, hear his father's stories and lead him around by the hand.

The last little spark of the sun had already expired a long time before Mandel and Maruschka returned to the room. They lit a candle and found Amadeus still in his usual place at the table. He was lying with his head on his arms and looking straight ahead out of large, still eyes. Maruschka stepped up to him to take him to bed. At her affectionate, formless sounds, he started softly. Then he shut his eyes and could no longer be convinced to open them.

4

That evening Amadeus lay awake until the light was extinguished. For he wanted to look out to see if Maruschka would fly up to heaven.

The blue night stood outside and the moonlight lay on the window. And he kept looking into it, into the white shimmer.

Quite far off, he saw golden, trembling branches swaying up and down. They certainly came from the angels waving to his mute mother that she should go up. Now the branches began to turn, at first slowly, then ever faster until they became a flashing whirlwind. Finally they had bored a circular, golden door in the blue heaven. It gradually climbed higher and a silvery white road flowed forth from it, down the night, through the window into the room.

On the floor above him, steps could be heard, wavering down the stairs, and when they reached the door, it opened by itself. Marushka entered soundlessly. She had a long, dragging garment on and was leading two white goats by her side. Amadeus held his breath. The goats snuffed at the floor as if searching for stalks. But when they came to the shiny silver road which hung down from heaven into the room, they climbed up on their hind legs. His mute mother became tall and travelled up the sparkling road through the window and into the night. A roaring followed behind her. It was soon over the roof and finally ceased humming in the maple.

Then the white path to heaven lay quite solitary there again, and it looked just as if it were flowing continuously. The little door in the high, blue night outside did not become smaller or darker, even as so much silver pathway was still shooting forth from it. No, a sudden flash even twitched sometimes between the posts of the heavenly entrance, and every time a joyful fright travelled through Amadeus because he thought his other mother would now soon appear and glide down through the window to him. But he waited and waited in vain, and the darkness crept from all the corners of the room ever thicker around the silvery path and swallowed it. How easily the shadow could grasp even more strongly and pull more firmly so that the white path was thereby torn asunder. Then his mother did not find her way to him through the blackness and he had to lie in bed all alone. It overwhelmed him so that he screamed out with all his strength. Eusebius, whose bed stood in the other corner, finally heard him and came to him to calm him down. Amadeus clasped his father and whimpered incessantly, "My mother. The goats." When the tailor had drawn the curtains, the little boy fell asleep.

Late the next morning, since Christoph's work was already under way in the bright sunlight, the mute stepped up to Amadeus's bed and woke him. The little boy turned around quickly and, when he saw Maruschka before him, his face froze in an expression which was half surprise and half dismay. Then he shoved the woman's hands away when they tried to stroke his forehead, and looked around the room help-lessly. Maruschka was clothed in the same skirt as ever, his father was sitting and sewing, and the golden branches which had bored a little door into heaven were also no longer to be seen. Only the window stood wide open and the song of the larks rang into the room. 'Aha,' thought Amadeus, 'while I was sleeping, my mute mother fled into the house again. But then the two goats must also be home again.' He quickly clambered out of bed and ran as he was over to the goats' stall. The two animals stood in the half darkness at the back by the wall and turned their heads to him. But he did not be-lieve it. Around the two goats which had sprung into heaven the previous night, there had been a bright shimmer. The other two before him in the stall had rough hair which lay all tangled up. They were angry an-imals which thrust with their horns and now, since he did not come to them, they were bleating needlessly and noisily and climbing with their forelegs onto the fodder rack as if they wanted to break away from their tethers and charge at him. Amadeus fled, as hurriedly as his little legs could carry him, into the house and cowered in the backmost corner. There he shut his eyes and waited apprehensively for what would happen now.

Eusebius saw that his boy seemed to be hounded by something unseen, that not everything was right with him, and when he did not intervene for a long time, Amadeus was still looking around with such timid eyes, leaning against the wall motionless for minutes with a pale face and then being startled to tears when he was called. In the end, this elven fragility became to much for him, and if the child could not tie a knot in good time, it would in the end become accustomed to such weaving in the air because it thought it beautiful and would botch its future even before it could begin. For that reason, the tailor enforced that Amadeus, after dressing and washing, came in orderly train to the foot-stool for his breakfast. There he then applied himself attentively to the little pot and the bread. Actually too cautiously and measured, his head bowed, almost like an old man. And Eusebius thought to himself, 'a strong boy; he has everything from me! And he purses his lips again so happily when he is wetting the threads to lead them through the eye.' Then nobody worried anymore about the boy who had stopped eating. His little hands lay before him on the chair and his little head was still bowed. Only, from time to time, he looked out from under his brow. For the room there before him, everything in it, and even his entire life had become quite alien to him. The stove had a terrible yawning gap at its base, from which the thousands of men from Berlin had formerly travelled forth and journeyed with great noise over the rooves. Today nothing but an old boot of his father's was in it and its top was hanging down to the side. The footstool stuck its stiff legs woodenly against the floor and had formerly been a horse with which he could ride to Hamburg or Halle. The tin funnel did not blow so loudly anymore so that you had to jump if you only looked at it, and the bulbous jug which had previously marched as a stout woman up and down in the pot cupboard, stretched its snout out rigidly and did not stir, as if it were quite dead.

Amadeus became hard of breath in this hidden strangeness. In addition, thick mist outside was edging itself suddenly around the tailor's house and the sun lay in it so that Mother Hulda's feathers shimmered golden here and there. Through every window, pale golden strands of light flowed into the room and hung trembling in the air like string on which someone was playing; always four next to each other, exactly as many as there were panes in the window. Amadeus listened for what sort of music would ensue from them, but it remained quiet. Sometimes the golden strings just climbed to the ceiling or sank to the floor. When the boy saw that, the silver road on which Maruschka had flown to heaven the previous night occurred to him, and he thought, 'if it doesn't stop, it could go so far that my father also goes out the window.' But he behaved calmly, closed his eyes and listened, because he wanted to hear the ringing of the golden branches with which the angels lured men from the earth. After he had been sitting in his night like that for a while, it began to wander over quite far away, as soft and as high as the tones of a small bell. But the closer the sounds came to him, the more they were mixed up with a rustling and finally sank entirely into it so that in the end, only a noise like that of the wind blowing a person's clothes was in his ears. Then Amadeus became scared to the depth of his soul, for he thought it had now seized his father and was carrying him out the window.

That's why he quickly opened his eyes again and looked to his father at the cutting table. What he saw there was appalling. A little, gaunt man was crouching there. His large head with its long nose was hanging down deeply. Every second a jerk ran through his thin body and then it seemed every time as if it were not a man at all, let alone his father, but a great, black bird pecking without interruption at something. Nobody else was to blame but Martin Schallke for his father becoming so dissimilar, because he had trampled him with his feet the day before. He began to ache within and ached more and more over what would happen if he had a great, black bird for a father. In the end, he could not endure it anymore. He called with failing voice to his father and at the same time, let his eyes close in fear again. Before he could repeat the call once more, steps were stumbling across the floor to him. He felt a damp hand stroke his cheek and at the same time, a chirping voice spoke, "What is it then, Amadeus? Hey, tell me, what is it with you for God's sake?"

The boy shook all over. For his true father, before the Schnallke boy had trampled over him, had soft, warm hands and his voice had sounded as if the sun were singing over them in the still summer air. For that reason, he was frightened of looking at the transformed man. After many requests, little Mandel finally dared to lead his eyes into the light. There he saw his father for the first time as he was: a thin, crooked little man in a greasy jacket which hung on sloping shoulders. With long, wizened fingers, he now grasped his little son's hand and chirped, pressing them affectionately, "Such a devil of a fellow! What sort of nonsense you have in your head."

Then he went to his cutting table again and continued flittering. But Amadeus was still so astonished by the incomprehensible turbidity of life that he did not have the confidence to move, because he thought that then something even worse could perhaps happen. The beams of the ceiling hung as though they would fall down any moment. Maruschka had gone to heaven and no longer went constantly in and out from one moment to the next, and he could not work out whether she was his mother or not. Of his father, he did not know exactly if he was journeying halfway around the world with the King of Prussia or the Schnallke boy had transformed him into a black bird or he was just a stooped tailor. It all afflicted him so much that he had to spring up and run out.

There the clouds were flying in the sky. The twisted willow was beating with its long branches as if it would like for all its life to journey with them up into the air. The wind threw the birds into the air as if they were little stones, and the trees stooped and caught them. But everything Amadeus saw there happened far away from him, like in another land, and he could not even arrive there with his eyes. For that reason, he sat down on the little bench next to the door and waited for everything that he had once had to return to him.

Only it turned into evening and did not change. His father's voice rang strangely through the wall. The Hainwald forest stood blue up above and moved further and further into the meadow so that you could barely distinguish its trunks anymore, and Amadeus thought, 'The forest is wandering away, and when it disappears I will be utterly, utterly alone.' Just then, as he pondered that, he saw high in the sky a murder of crows turning. Above the maple under which he sat, they wheeled around a few times, and in their midst was one who would have liked to have flown down and settled on a branch, but the others tore at it with loud cries so that it desisted and floated into the heights with the others until they all disappeared in the treetops of the forest. Perhaps his father had indeed become a bird and wanted to come down again to his house. But the others would not allow it and had taken him away with themselves.

That clenched Amadeus's chest so much that he would have died from lack of breath if he had not started singing. He let his eyes close and put his entire soul into his voice. It led him cautiously out of his fear into the world which he had not yet seen, and when he sang, regardless of what it was, sky or clouds or forest or his father or his mother, everything became as it had been and yet much, much more beautiful.

Finally, when it had already become quite dark and the time for going to sleep had arrived, the tailor Mandel stepped out to his son and asked what the beautiful thing he was singing was. But Amadeus could not say what had happened to him, instead he flung his arms around his father's neck and squeezed him close.

5

The little door through which our life slips in sleep into dreaming has such low and narrowly placed posts that of the noisy and broad burden of the day, only the most secret, most precious things which lie right next to the heart can find entry.

Thus the hardship and sorrow of Amadeus over his father, over his mother, the entire heavy worry because of the strangeness of his life remained lying on the threshold of sleep, and his bare, sweet little soul took with it into the dream none of the events of that evening when he had with his voice drawn the whole world into himself. The long night became a single journey through colourful transformations: sometimes he flew above the treetops of a blue forest; sometimes he floated so closely over the meadow that the flowers touched him; sometimes he lay without a wish lost in the highest part of the heavens, and nothing was around him but the light of the sun. It ran down constantly to him like a endless, golden stream. But everything he grazed in flight, touched with his hands, or even encompassed with his look, rang out like a harp through whose strings the wind was skimming. All things emerged from the taciturnity of their being, and the gestures of their shapes, and their colours revealed themselves to him in tones which were like an audible transfiguration around them.

On awakening the next morning, however, this ringing tether which had bound him to everything had been torn, and with seeing eyes, the consciousness of its mysterious power sank back into him. The little dream door closed in front of his soul and he stood like the day before in a confusion of inexplicably taciturn things with which nothing bound him but an expectation of a resounding colourfulness which slumbered enchanted in everything.

And Amadeus would perhaps have suffered dark wonder for a row of difficult days if Mandel, directed by the unease of his boy, had not recalled his promise to him and thereby prepared an end to the sewing in the air, as he called it in his mind.

The next morning, Amadeus found next to his little pot of milk the present from his father, through which his wandering would be bound, a slate and a neatly sharpened pen lying on it. With quiet earnesty, forgetting hunger and thirst, he went about the examination of this equipment, placed the slate on the little pot and let it be a roof under which he shoved two horses and a wagon, all broken from the piece of bread. Eusebius crept from his work and gave the appearance of an overzealous man. In truth he was peering hard at his boy and thinking, 'Now we'll see if a gentleman resides in him.' Of course he had anticipated that Amadeus would instantly seize the pen and write the entire ABC and still more on the slate, and his expectation made his soul fairly ache. When he saw him lean the slate against the chair as a wall, he made two long, deep stitches in cheerful bafflement whilst saying to himself, "The peach deliberates like an old man!" The thing with the roof which then came next again did not seem clear to Eusebius and he cleared his throat. But when the future gentleman now led the hunks of bread with whoa and giddy-up back and forth under the roof, old Mandel let the farrier's jacket fall, went over and instructed his little son in the use of the slate and the pen, placed his little fingers around the pen and guided his hand up and down. Thus proper mountains appeared on the slate and Amadeus delighted in everything tucked in the pen. Finally his father showed him how to write an 'i', and whenever he was finishing it and came to the point, he called out the name of the letter, long and with a cheerfully drawn out voice so that it sounded not unlike a crow's cry.

"Is that a hen?" Amadeus asked after watching a few times.

"Why a hen?" was his father's disconcerted counter-question and he realised that he felt a little bit aggrieved.

"Because it cries like the farmer Schnallke's young, white hen", Amadeus answered and did not know how to explain why there was an angry trembling about his father's nose as though from mice's feet.

"A hen!" Eusebius finally cried out scornfully, "A hen! It is a letter, boy, take note!"

Amadeus looked for the envelope and found none, and because his father had spoken so gruffly, the boy did not dare say anything more.

After breakfast the little boy got stuck into writing the 'i'. But they were funny things which came out of the pen when you took it in hand and pressed on it. It clambered about on every line, hung sometimes up in a corner and crept sometimes down into an angle. Now they lay flat like the children in front of Hildesheim's wall, now they stood upright like a belltower. If you looked at the pot and then let the pen run, it travelled all around and it became what it comprehended. The thin slate pen knew the stove and the chair, the table and the funnel. Amadeus found no end at all to trying the magic which was hidden in the pen. As an incomprehensible guide, it led the little boy back to the secrecy of all things. And whenever he got up to go do something else, he heard the pen very softly pecking as if it was calling to him. If Amadeus then looked over, it lay there as still as it had slid from his hand; but as soon as he held it between his fingers, something else was already flowing out from it again. Nothing remained hidden to the pen. Through the door, it could see into the hallway. It knew what was in the stalls without having to look through the window, it drew everything that was in the world outside. Slowly it also liberated the people who slept in the things. The little dream door to Amadeus's soul was opening. The ringing tether which had bound him that evening with everything distant went forth from it radiantly, and the resounding transfiguration which had slumbered in the earth's being was opened up in the heart of the little, pale, tailor's boy. He made the crows emerge through the blue of the approaching night and hold dialogues in the air. His other mother came to him, travelling from heaven on the sparkling road; his father was neither a black bird nor a bent over little man, but was wandering about with the King of Prussia again, and everything that Amadeus drew, he sang with a soft, tinkling voice.

Eusebius often stood up and looked over his shoulder at the rapt boy without being able to comprehend how the lines and rings which confusedly covered the slate could bring such wondrous things into his soul and such never-heard-before songs from his lips.

Then he sat down at his place again and was often incapable of stirring his hands to the accustomed industry. For the singing of his boy broke the spell of silence and muteness which had long held shackled his past. Colourful veils climbed from forgotten pits and lights gleamed out of the darknesses of his life. The Hainwald forest, through which his wife had travelled never to be seen again, veiled itself in a shimmer, and once he even saw Agathe herself emerge from the shadow of the trees, as she had been: her head bowed so that her long, peaceful face could not be seen under the ribboned bonnet. The prayer book pressed to her breast with still hand and the skirt stirring slowly with her steady, peaceful gait. Thus she strode from there, as Mandel had seen her approach his little house probably a thousand times before from this window. But when he bent forward with pounding heart to more accurately perceive the apparition, it all disappeared into nothing. Only the sunlight trembled for a while more golden over the place she had been.

From this vision, it became clear to Eusebius from whom Amadeus had received the many songs with which he was filling the little tailor's house under the maple by Upper Röhrsdorf. Agathe had once sung just as softly and gently when Mandel, as a young fellow lying behind a corn field, had waited on her for a pleasure stroll through the meadows. In that period of time, before his eyes, red, sparkling streams had also travelled across the ears with her wandering, wistful singing. At a later time, in the toil of life, the singing had faded and withered in her mouth; only in her eyes did a deeper tone reside unconquerably which was only extinguished with her death. Now his wife's soul, that which had been buried in her distant youth, was singing from the mouth of her little son so that it often seemed to him as if everything were as beautiful as before and no horror had ever touched his little house, nor his heart either which crouched in his chest like an un-fledged chick in its nest, happy and extremely restive because the world was opening up before it.

For that reason, Eusebius did not plague his son any-more with the 'i'; for he thought, 'If Amadeus did not become "a man of the court" then, anyway, a thousand paths on earth led to a golden end when every piece in the head sat in the right place.'

6

Thus Christoph Eusebius Mandel enjoyed for some time full of satisfaction that his little son was wandering about the world with his pen, as he once had with his walk-ing stick, and skewering what seemed remarkable to him. The little room rang day in, day out with the songs of the child's voice, and everything young, colourful and cher-ished which had ever laughed, shimmered and been sought after in this room, had been sleeping in the darkness of a narrow corner for a long time and rested forgotten in its rough walls, awoke from its accursedness and became un-real pictures on that veil for whose sake life is so precious to men. The roof ridge repeated the song like an indis-tinctly subsiding echo, and the wind playing before the windows carried it up to the twisted willow which thus bowed just a little deeper and trembled at the same time with its long roots as if thinking of its own youth.

Everything had its bright joy in the drawing singer who often seemed to have penetrated so deeply into the autocratical wonder of the song that he no longer used the pen's images anymore on his path into the resounding transfiguration, but found his way in jots, like in tiny footsteps, into the play of sounds and out again. The little dream door into Amadeus's soul did not close anymore. It became wider and ever wider, and finally the boy resided with his pale face only in those pleasures which men who are born on a Trinity Sunday experience of the world. From far away, the song strolled into his mouth, from distances where powers are at work which can grasp no thought, exhaust no word.

Since it had been unbound, had become only sound, colour and light, Amadeus's song was even digging up depths in Christoph Eusebius's soul which old Mandel possessed no power over. He waited in vain for his boy's song to conjure up once again the image of his wife out of the Hainwald forest. It seem extinguished in him and buried forever. And even if he still tried so hard and employed several tricks, he only ever came in his memory to the point where he had waited as a young fellow in the country lane for Agathe. The more often he faltered at this image and was caught with his mood in the magic of that distant time, the more inescapably he was captured as though in a circle of fire. Yes, many a time he forgot completely that, as an old man whose hair was already flecked with grey at the temples, he was crouching on hard wood in his narrow room, and it seemed to him that he was really lying outside under the summer hot sky and the ripe corn was waving with a gentle rustling around him. Then Agathe's song wandered from his little son's mouth to him like it had then. But the sounds which met him in such moments were not the wistfully mild ones he longed for. It wafted a fierce fervour into him which he had to choke down like a lustful asphyxiation.

Then it tempted him away from his work and led him on a gentle walk across the floor. His feet forgot that they had already become hard and stiff in the arduous path of forty eight years and alternated in high spirits between the traditional steps of a Scottish reel or the shuffling of an Austrian folk dance. A quite excessive spirit often seized him as well. He fell with a crowing high voice into Amadeus's song and marched with sawing arms in such a bold pose through the room as if he had decided to add a new, outrageous adventure to his many-sided career and hike directly to Russia or, if possible, to Turkey.

Attracted by such merriment, mute Maruschka herself stepped up to the little singer, lit herself up from his rapturous face and his shimmering look, and sucked the gesture of his tones from his mouth with her eyes. In this way, the ungovernable youth also streamed into her full, voluptuous body so that she was no longer strolling about oppressed by her eternal silence, heavy and dazed. She straightened her shoulders. Her face glowed. Her eyes obtained a youthful brilliance. Her steps became free and firm so that the floorboards bent under the burden of her body.

But as soon as Maruschka appeared in the room, old Mandel took refuge with his jacket and looked furtively and shyly at her blossoming. The hot haze from his boy's song befogged his head like a gentle vertigo. And the face of his mute housekeeper then assumed the features of his Agathe, her dress flowing as with hers around her step, a scent like ripe grain rushing at him, and his heart constricted fearfully at the thought that the woman could approach him and make a little tap on his back, as was her way, to ask him with the play of her bare arms why he was cowering so soberly over the old jacket.

Thus the two older people were woven together by the boy's song and, without Amadeus needing to turn around, he knew whom his song was moving behind his back: sometimes his tones were inspired by passionate, glimmering exuberance, sometimes a dark, violent thing streamed controlling and heavily into them, depending on whether his father or Maruschka came into his purview.

Then one day, something strange took place which caused an end to Amadeus's singing for a long time.

Usually the little wagon of sleep transports us with a hard jolt to the edge of reality, and we are thrown into the day as if with a kick. But on the morning of that day, which would become so momentous for the Mandel house under the maple, because the fate of all the people who lived in it took a strange step, the little drawing singer was lifted without waking into the world of light. Every object appeared to be behind glassy, transparent water, unsteady, faltering and distant, and Amadeus himself did not feel settled in his bed, but rather sitting on a wave with which he swished into the depths when he closed his eyes, which breathed it in as soon as he raised his lids.

His father had left his bed before him. Already neatly ordered, the grey striped cover stroked smooth over the billowing feather pillows, it looked in the corner like a flatbed wagon from which the horses had been unharnessed. Old Mandel had climbed quietly from his bed into his clothes as if because of a danger, he had to creep to his day's work and even now, as he provided the last touches to his completed outfit before the small mirror on the wall, he acted stooped and silent. With painful exactness, he distributed the sparse, greying strands of hair over his bulbously raised forehead. At the same time, he turned back and forth to check the difficult work from all sides for its successfulness. After all that had been concluded to his satisfaction, he put the comb aside in the little woven straw casket under the mirror with a smacking sound from his lips, wet the palms of his hands with spit and brushed his trousers down. This was his way of ending every fitting out, even

if this was never, with the exception of Sunday and festive days, so thoroughly practised.

Amadeus followed everything with the attentiveness
of the early awoken and with the astonishment which
was still caught in his eyes from his dream. He saw his
father far away in a vagueness so that he thought it
would be impossible to reach him with his voice. And
yet he would have liked to have called him; but he was
scared to speak because he would have had to make his
words so thin and timid in order to drill them out to
that distance.

Only, when he saw his father brushing his trousers
down eagerly and noticed how he then stepped excitedly
from one window to the next, murmured in tumbling
sounds and drew his shoulders up at the same time, did
Amadeus have an apprehension that something special
was planned. Perhaps he could even be wanting to
travel away. For that reason, the little boy plucked up
his courage and spoke through the glassy water at old
Mandel, "Where are you wanting to go, father?"

The tailor, rapt, self-absorbed, thought his little son
was still sleeping. Now, as he was met by his timid
voice, he turned around abruptly and crowed cheerfully,
"Oh, you are already out of the feathers! — Me, little
Amadeus, off? — Oh no, I don't want to go anywhere.
Not to Russia and not to Turkey."

"But why are you in such a wide water and brushing
your trousers like it is Sunday?" the boy asked and hesitated, perplexed.

"It isn't water, it's air. It doesn't ripple. See! Well?!"
the tailor spoke effervescently and threw his arms in all
directions to heal his little son from the conceits. "You
are such a funny boy! You must wake up with the right
eye, not with the left one. Otherwise the entire day will
end up contrary."

Then he approached hastily with his uneven, somewhat skipping steps, took the child's chin in his thumb and forefinger, turned his face up to him and spoke encouragingly into his questioning eyes, "Look at your father, he is a fellow, understand! If Mr Gufernement were to take a look at me, ha, he would be wide-eyed! For in Russia, it happens, my boy, that you sometimes aren't steady in your own boots. Then you can't stride out for long before you unexpectedly end up head over heels. Then you must, oops, out and about, understand. But I'll tell you about that another time. Now get up and be very good. Got it, Amadeus?"

With that he abruptly left the little one and began, contrary to his usual habit, a zealous, restive housekeeping in the room, in the house and in the little garden without actually achieving anything. In his limitless head, a whirl of images was fermenting. And while he skipped up and down in his room in Upper Röhrsdorf, he thought he was girding himself in a broad hall for a dangerous undertaking. The meadow in the hot morning haze transformed into an endless plain through which a confusion of paths scurried, back and forth, and he did not know which he should pursue and to where he should turn. The Hainwald forest stood blurry in the morning haze like a spread out, foreign city. Trees tailed off into thousands of towers, house gables, chimneys and flag poles in the smoky heights. But everywhere his excited imagination led him, he scented an important, implacable person to whom an incomprehensible concern was pushing him and before whom he must at the same time be on his guard.

Amadeus had not followed his instructions to leave his bed, but sat in his bed with his shirt drawn over his knees.

Sometimes Maruschka skimmed past him: reddened, heavy and strong, so that everything shook and the plates in the pot cupboard rattled softly; sometimes Christoph Eusebius took refuge from the Russian plain in his dwelling only to be driven out again by his timidity before this transformed space. By this aimless, impassioned wandering, his father became almost as strange to him as when he had once been a bird, and every missed step took him a step further away from him. Then the glassy, transparent airy water condensed more and more and finally enshrouded old Mandel as if in rays.

"My father is now in Russia", Amadeus thought because he could not explain the incomprehensible thing in any other way.

Then he left his bed and not long after was sitting again in front of the chair by the window, his accustomed dreamer's place. For he longed for a beautiful song from the unease which had closed in on him from his father. But even outside, he found no foothold. The air was a hot, silvery white trembling, a restive, twitching veil behind which every object looked half blown away. Only the blue of the distant mountain forest erected itself dark and certain into the pale blue sky.

When Amadeus let his glance rest on this beautiful darkness, the magnificence, breathing quite softly, struck off heavy, velvety tones somewhere and skimmed past his ears like the wind-blown arpeggio of a distant aeolian harp. But as soon as a ray of the sun emerged over the forest or his father entered the room, the ringing died away and was not to be caught, even if he pressed his little hands to his eyes and crept into the darkness within himself. He perceived nothing but the gesture of the wandering tones, only they were behind gauze, and he only felt its soundless rhythm beating against his heart.

"Father, I can't get the song", he finally said reproachfully to Christoph Eusebius who had just fled from the foreign city into the room again.

"Which song?" old Mandel asked absentmindedly and stepped over to him.

"Well, the song which is in the blackness and behind the long bush", the child answered.

But the tailor was entangled too deeply in the whirl of images which was driving his seething blood into his brain. He murmured something unintelligible under his breath and riveted his eyes in impatiently fearful expectation onto the door which he had locked behind himself for safety, even though a motionless heat lay in the room.

At this moment, Amadeus heard steps heading through the grass towards the house and saw how his father, who must have been listening too, paled as a result, bowed before something invisible and began stutteringly to speak, "You will forgive me," he said, "Mr Gufernement, that I, and I take the liberty of joining with you. I am just a simple tailor, but ..." Only he could not play to an end the scene of reception, veiled in the impregnable imagination of his quest, for Maruschka stepped erect, broad and sturdy into the room. Her eyes were smouldering again with an unusual brilliance. Her arms were blossoming in brown freshness and a subjugating, tantalising current ran out from her. It closed in on the delicate boy too so that something like fear overcame him, for his mute mother had never appeared so strong and violent to him, and while he was moving back a little on his little footstool to get out of her purview, he noticed how his father also climbed to his cutting table and blinked from there at Marushka, as pallor and redness ran across his face.

"Mr Gufernement ... Mr Gufernement ... Mr Gufernement ..." he murmured constantly, submissively —
begging — hot — stifled.

A nameless trembling then seized Amadeus, and he
was no longer capable of looking into the room, which
was filled with menace and oppressiveness. But hardly
had his glance again met the deep blue of the mountain
forest behind the trembling of the air, than it smashed
to pieces like the rustling of great, fiery wings over him,
the gauze of his soul was torn up and, like a singing
flame, the yearned for song sprang up in him. At first it
was long, avid screams which he had to sing. Then his
song became a play of sunlit, quick wings over treetops
deep below. Finally it winged forth like a passionate
plunge into the void until it was wavering with stutteringly sweet sounds before a gate in which the dance of
heavy shadows was turning. And while he was suffering
so in the magic of the song from which he was being
carried, he sensed how behind him the sounds lifted his
father from the cutting table and led him across the
floor, closer and closer to something dark, violent, suck-
ing him in. The boy's voice almost lost itself before that
which was threatening his father and his song. But he
was not capable of seeking refuge from the spell. It sub-
jugated him to such an extent that his song finally
dissipated into an impassioned coughing.

In this extreme affliction of rapture, he felt a blow
pass through his body, like that which jolts through us
when the wagon we are sitting on stops suddenly after a
long, quick trip. Abruptly and achingly, the song collapsed in him. Exhausted, as though in rapture,
Amadeus sat for a while as if he had awoken from a
heavy dream.

Finally he ventured to turn around. There he saw his
father nestled hard against his mute mother who was
holding him with glowing face like a defenceless quarry

in her strong hands. The tailor's fingers lay buried in the flesh of her arms. He was pale, bearing an expression of deep anguish in his face and trembling as if chilled.

The tears entered the boy's eyes because Maruschka had played so wickedly with his father. He stood up, detached Mandel's hand from the woman's arm and dragged him out of the room. The tailor was incapable of words and left the house with his boy. Both walked across the little strip of meadow to the twisted willow. There they sat down and looked for a long time, without saying a word, into the little stream which ran through the grass in front of them.

In the end, Christoph Eusebius gathered his breath, stroked his son's forehead and said, asking timidly, "Amadeus, is it true you won't sing anymore?"

The boy did not dare to look up and just nodded sorrowfully.

His father crept away from him, bent over and depressed, to the little bench behind the house where you could see the Upper Röhrsdorf path running into the Hainwald forest. There he remained, without asking for food and drink, as if deaf and dumb, until it was pitch black.

7

The next day, the tailor Mandel nevertheless bestrode his bench from one moment to the next and waxed the threads as if nothing had happened.

You could admittedly hang the success of the work on a nail driven into the air, and if old Mandel seemingly still plied away as boisterously, his needle just skipped upwards without pricking; but this bustling was not reigning over him out of embarrassment, rather he was executing it with meaningful intent.

The master had intended to no longer think of the events of the previous day and to go his usual way in peace. And that was the only means for straightening out the whole story. For matters that crouch in ambush on us have their own background. They ride us for a while. But if you cast them off for a moment when their grizzling slackens for a while and decide to slam the door behind you, they usually stand for a while yet and wait for you to find your way back to them. But when you remain stubbornly on the spot to which deliberation has assigned us, then they will surely scrape at the door like impatient beggars, look with red faces through the window as if you were guilty of something, and then gradually disappear so that you are undisputed master in your house again.

Eusebius pondered it while his needle was swooping in the air all the time, and the firmer he stitched together to such an extent this resolution, the more surely he came into his former disposition.

Yes, everything would have found itself in the old position again in the tailor's house if Maruschka had not been there. When she walked across the room, a white wafting drew through the air, somewhere a ringing unleashed itself, and whether the master wanted to or not, he had to crouch down and follow the blossoming woman with wide eyes.

Even Amadeus paid attention with an unmistakeable trembling when the mute woman came into the vicinity of his father, and watched to see if the trembling would pass over his body and the pale anguish come into his face again like the day before.

These disturbances whose avoidance did not lie in the tailor's hand heated up the Mandels' room so that Eusebius realised he had to throw himself on another horse if he wanted to ride in honour from this watering place to which he had come.

The forester on Rimberg mountain had some time before said something to him about the dilapidated state of his uniform. If he met him still at home, perhaps a deal could be made.

Without hesitating for long, Mandel climbed from the cutting table, began undressing while striding back and forth and rehearsing his introduction in the forester's house.

Thus: he knocked. — Good morning, forest ranger! — Morning, master! What in heavens brings you up here? — You know, forest ranger, swallows and tailors have the same fondness. — Well, and in what way? — Well, they don't suffer the low eaves. They like most of all to be high up. Yes, that's why I have come up to you just now ... and so on. You could call him Hans, not Christoph Eusebius, if he did not make the forester a uniform like no other that had hung in a ranger's wardrobe as long as Rimberg had existed: military! Pluck! A cut for snatching!

That's right, Mandel wanted to wangle it like that. These colourful puffs made his soul seeth while he finished with restless wandering the preparations for departure.

In the end, he stood in the middle of the room and assessed which stick he should take, the one of mountain hazel with the carved handle or the shiny bamboo one with the beautiful Melton colour. He decided on the latter, the more dressy walking equipment, because he considered that nothing introduced a craftsman, especially a tailor, to his customers better than an obtrusive nobility in appearance. For this reason, he also hung the green fleece back in the cupboard, put on his black spencer and topped it with the semi-stiff felt hat.

Thus equipped, he beckoned Maruschka, and when she was standing before him, as always with her plump arms entwined acquiescently below her high breasts and her glance directed observantly at her master's mouth, the entire Russian story seemed to Eusebius to be an unimportant tale and his unrest up to the previous evening as an absurdly descending haze.

If a hole had been bored into the hidden needle box of his inner being, he would not have now been, as he stood and looked at her, so button cool. No, no! And if nevertheless a little weed's seed had smuggled into him with Amadeus's song, he could tear it out straightaway with the first little shoot.

He was not at a loss for a reason. He straightened up, laid his hand on his defective hip, set his foot forward a little and then said in condescending, but absolutely serious tones, "The beets in the garden are full of salt-bush."

Maruschka looked at him perplexed and then broke out into mocking laughter.

Mandel did not let himself be put off his stride and repeated firmly, "Saltbush!"

And when the mute, instead of being shattered by the serious steadfastness of the tailor, repeated her laughter only more amused, the master cut a pair of razor-sharp lips and said threateningly, "Saltbushes, dumb wench, saltbushes!" With that he struck her a blow suggestively with his open hand on her bare upper arm. "I will show you!"

Then he went out with her, leant on the garden fence and, although the beets displayed not a spit of weed, he laughed insultingly in the mute woman's now pale, pinched face, gestured with his hand over everything and said ruthlessly, "If I say to you saltbush, then there is saltbush! Take note once and for all." Then he swivelled uprightly onto the road through the village to the Rimberg and further.

Behind the first houses, he paused a few times, sought out a small stone on the path, struck down on it with his stick and laughed in mocking triumph at the same time.

The tailor, nevertheless, did not make it to the Rimberg for his great business.

At first he went to the small trader in yarns who ran his tiny business at the end of the village a bit to the side in a little depression amongst fruit trees. He sat with him on the bench and listened to the news which the beardless, infinitely skinny man babbled with a high, singing voice. From the flax miller, he learnt that the forester was constructing paths at the furthest limit of his district and would not be back home before evening. He lingered here for quarter of an hour and then climbed, lapsing into a distracted mood, to the Rimberg anyway. A singing in which the voices of the small trader and Amadeus intwined together was running next to the tailor.

"Where are you going then? The forester isn't home", the miller shouted to him.

"So I already know the path when I have to go up it again", Eusebius called back, and both men laughed.

Half way up there was a tavern under two massive lime trees, and a path led between barn and residence out into the fields and then gradually climbed up the steep slope until it narrowed at the edge of a forest clearing into a foot track and ran along under wild cherry trees.

The high, singing trader's voice through which an indeterminable drunkenness bleated did not fade away from the tailor's ears. Sometimes it seemed as if the thin, beardless man was walking on his left, sometimes on his right side. Breathless from the quick climb, bathed in sweat from the heat, almost dizzy from this "trader's chatter", Eusebius arrived under the cherry trees. He sat down in the shade, took his hat off, cooled his face with his colourful handkerchief and relinquished himself a little to the pleasures of rest. But as soon as his eyes closed, there was a jolt and it seemed to Eusebius as if the mountain was falling through the air. He started and looked across the meadow to find out who it had been. There he saw a dancing girl who immediately vanished in such passionate whirling between the bushes that her dress flew up far above her calves. Mandel quickly wiped his eyes to see better; but then he saw nothing but two young birch trees waving their crowns on white trunks.

The tailor sprang up with curses on the trader, stamped down angrily down on a cluster of tansies and set off again. Towards evening he found himself exhausted and famished, without a good idea of the success of his business trip, at the Sauerborn mill. It was also a stopping place.

The miller's wife, clean and tidy as ever, curious and trusting as was her art, beset Eusebius over where he had come from and why he was in his Sunday attire. But she got nothing out of him. The depressed little man bit eagerly into the bread and cheese and drank the glass of simple beer in one gulp. At the same time, he looked out the window in a sort of entranced sorrow. When the miller's wife became to much of a nuisance with her questions and chatter, he stuffed a few quickly snatched lies into her ears. At the approach of darkness, he set off on the three quarter hour long way home. Already in darkness, he came to the path which led from the mountain houses to near his house. At the bush behind

Schnallke's farm, he paused and listened. In his house, a window must be open; for, when he held his breath, he could hear his Amadeus singing: at first softly, as though begging, then quiet trilling like a gentle breeze shaking golden blond hair. Eusebius remained motionless where he was as long as the song lasted. It scurried past quickly and finished with sounds of such gentle ardency that each tone ran down the back of the master like a seething trickle.

In the house, by comparison, everything already lay in deepest peace. Amadeus was sleeping, one arm shoved under his head, and smiling in dream.

Old Mandel felt entirely as if bewitched, leant his bamboo stick in the corner and shook his head.

On the next and following days, the tailor Eusebius did not leave his Sunday attire and his restive undertakings.

When the first cockcrow sprang from Schnallke's farm, it served to sweep an entire village behind its brow. He was always the first on his feet in the Mandel house, made himself ready to leave and asked for his breakfast. He ignored his housekeeper's astonishment completely. While the mute woman plied away diligently at the stove, he stood at the window and looked out pondering. He then drank his coffee hastily, stuck fashion pages in the side pockets of his coat and set off.

But everytime he turned back after the first hundred steps into the field and gave Maruschka instructions for the day: the goats were to be groomed; the grass must be scythed; the wood in the shed is stacked too carelessly. He said everything with decisiveness, and when the mute woman once asked with scornful gestures if the chimney should be brushed, he waved such an agitated answer into the air that it seemed as if he had not arms but sharply honed knives by his sides.

He climbed up to the mountain houses, passed through Ranser, a farming settlement below the long bush; strolled to Sauerborn, scattered farms which filled an abruptly inclined, charming gorge as though fleeing the world, and roamed about the Röhrsdorf farms too. Ever busy, ever breathless, the bamboo stick in his right hand, his hat in his left, the tailor trotted through the summer haze from farm to farm. He spread out his fashion pages, talked of the advantages of the newest garb, sought to convince here for a new suit, there for accommodating trousers or even just for a flowery vest, rolled out his measuring tape, unfolded his notebook, was inexhaustible in his praises and was constantly wetting the tip of his pencil with his tongue. It was no use. The women smiled covertly at his seams, the farmers called informal greetings to him across the fields when he was skipping lopsidedly along the field margins or let him taste darkly smouldering scorn when he sat himself down with them by the edge of the ditches and made his manouvres.

And every day old Mandel returned after dark, paused, observed his house expectantly from a distance and felt each evening more apprehensive when he always found everything dark, empty and silent.

For in him cowering behind shrouds was a hope for some sort of surprising, festive reception: resplendent voices, flying streamers, joyfully waving arms; but all this stuffed his chest full of apprehension and, at the same time, a deep ardency climbed screaming in him, like only the soul of a born tailor can endure. The yearning to find refuge in the unmeasured and unfettered drove him on these business trips in which the powerless man showed off in cartloads, spoke of great changes in his "metier" and, at the same time, made strange alterations. He wanted to bestride the times, embrace his fortune, kick his fate into tenuousness and pinch favour by the leg. And of all the colourful intoxication which he spun around himself during his restless day, nothing remained in the evening when he crept back timidly to his house but a buoyant fever, an enraptured sorrow hanging in his eyes.

The change in his father did not escape little Amadeus. In the short moments of the morning preparations for the "rounds", the boy had ample opportunity to be astonished by the twitching which ran continually over old Mandel's face and to be frightened by the anxiety which, sometimes as blanching, sometimes as shooting redness, fluttered over it. He saw him covertly twinkling at Maruschka and heard him speaking sharply and cutting to her before every departure. When he then saw his hat going down across the cornfields, the boy thought every time, 'Father is only doing it because of my Maruschka-mother.' He is still in Russia perhaps and she should not take him in her arms anymore so that he becomes sick and pale. With these thoughts, Amadeus felt close to his father, as if he were standing behind him, and heard him saying with quiet sorrow, "Amadeus, it's true you won't sing anymore." Then the boy let his songs fall silent, even when Eusebius was away. But most of all, the little one suffered from his father no longer hugging him and hardly speaking a word to him. Amadeus always planned to speak to him. But hardly had he put on an air to approach him than the tailor started, turned away unsettled or asked impatiently, "Well, what do you want again, little Amadeus?" Then the boy became tongue-tied, crept to the window and pressed his face against the panes so his forehead turned white. A little bunch of flowers his father had placed in an old mug on the cutting table was fading and, in the end, was tipped out and thrown away by Maruschka.

One day the master's ventures had already concluded in the early afternoon in the little birch forest through which the church path ran from Upper Röhrsdorf to Neudeck like a slowly dropped, grey frayed end.

Mandel did not exactly know how and why he had gone there. He lay down, sheltered by a hawthorn hedge from the eyes of passersby, a straw between his lips, and sometimes drummed his fingers on his hat which he had placed next to himself on the grass. Between the white trunks, he saw the seething hot summer haze trembling over the yellow expanse of ears, and sometimes here and there, a scythe flashed starkly from the ruffled waves. The reaper's sharpening sounded like the rubbing of steadfast crickets. At times a misshapen man's voice rumbled in the distance. The drowsy creaking of wheels drew through the country lanes.

"It will be a good harvest", Eusebius said softly and added, after losing himself in a long, sensual cloud of colourful dreams, "I will do it. Yes, yes, I am doing it."

On the path behind the hawthorn hedge, two men were just then walking past.

"Hey! — So? — And what have you done then?" asked a man's voice rough with excitation.

"What have I done?" a woman asked back snippily.

"Well yes." It sounded dull and cryptic.

"I've left him. What are you thinking of now, hey?" The woman laughed full of malicious contempt, though she seemed to him not quite honest. Then she continued, lapsing into rash babbling, "He had roamed about the house all the time. How can it be my fault if he ..."

The voices became indistinct and faded away down the slope.

Eusebius let the straw fall from his mouth, gathered up his hat and stick and wormed his way through the hawthorn hedge onto the path. But the pair had already disappeared behind a bend in the path and the tailor did not want to run after them. Furthermore, the day was already fast running out. For that reason, he ambled to the end of the little forest and looked raptly over Upper Röhrsdorf, whose farmsteads and houses were breathing a blue veil from their chimneys into the calm air over the shingle rooves playing in the evening red. He could not find the Mandel house. In the direction it must lie, a woman was standing on a hill and looking tensely to the road as if waiting for someone. The sinking sun hung straight above her over the long bush. Sharply outlined and black, she stood out like a super-human being against the red light, threatening and motionless.

The longer the tailor watched, the more irrefutably it obtruded on him that his house must lie in the area in which the woman was standing.

"Hey there, go away thank you. You there!" Christoph Eusebius called to himself. "My house isn't there so it can creep under your skirt."

As if the woman had heard the words he had cried in jesting annoyance, she now stretched her arms out to the side and described with them a few motions which looked like helplessness and longing.

Then he realised she was Maruschka.

At the same time, he heard resounding next to him the words of the woman whom he had eavesdropped on from behind the bushes, "He had roamed about the house all the time", and succumbed to a senseless fury which had lurked below the surface all the time just to spring up in him.

"Why has she run outside there? — If the goats have broken free! — Or a customer has come. — She's been lax again, with the entire house and Amadeus."

Mandel drilled into himself thus and struck furiously with his bamboo stick at the grass, a dog rose bush, and the green oats so that their grains clattered. He struck about blindly at whatever he could reach.

He waited until the twilight had set in and then crept, twisted like a corkscrew, into his house.

Everything was already dark again. Amadeus already lay in bed and was sleeping. Nobody, nobody awaited him. Everything was quiet, as if extinguished. The meal stood on the table as if for the first time.

Sighing, he hung his coat on the hook, stood a while in the middle of the room and heard nothing stirring. For that reason, he sat down perversely and ate.

But he devoured the meal heedlessly and hastily as if he still had to win some time for going to sleep, and continued to lie in wait with his ears meanwhile full of hidden, blind fury.

But nothing could be heard except the usual sounds of a summer night: the maple rustling cautiously over the roof; the little stream running its tiny, tinkling chimes incessantly into the meadow; a corn crake rasping through the hot, darkly lonesome field; and, now and then, the wind carrying from the distant forests a quiet hum through the window which sounded like the dreamy play of a double bass dropping off to sleep.

Then a strange noise mixed itself unexpectedly into the rapt concert of the summer night's darkness: a dull rattle, and sometimes it also sounded like the seething snorting of a large, dying animal, like the crying of a mute creature; abruptly breaking off, starting hesitantly and tailing off into high whimpering. Sometimes it sounded through the ceiling straight above the listening tailor, sometimes it seemed to come from the other corner of the house, tailing off into the wooden stalls, and now Mandel thought it was coming in from outside. It floated across the hallway to the living room door. Then it was extinguished completely and did not sound again. Eusebius heard it all, wedged between fear and recognition. By this disorderly, day long wandering and proliferation over the limits of his being, he found himself in a state of spirit in which he would have embraced it with prurient horror if the shadow of a deceased person had stepped through the door. For the Mandel house had become old in the strange fates of its inhabitants. The devil had once tripped the tailor's grandfather, the wagoner Mandel, beyond the Neudeck basin in a narrow gully which has since then been called the black stretch. Endless years of hardship and famine had pinched his father, the weaver Mandel, with soundless, merciless claws until he had died from the raw blaze of his hopes.

Who knows which of the two had been nocturnally driven out of the grave and through the house again. Eusebius stared at the wall for a long time to see whether he could see his father's weeping eyeballs as blood red stains there or whether perhaps the dead man would begin weaving on the chair in the attic. Nothing more was to be heard. For that reason, the tailor finally ventured with cautiously suppressed breath to clear the dishes from the table. Then he pulled himself fully together, locked the front door, shot the bolt across, checked each window and was so occupied with the prevention of possible danger that he did not notice how Amadeus was half upright in bed, watching everything and contemplating dreamily why his father, confined in a red sphere, was swinging continuously through the night. Then, as the tailor once more stepped to the boy's bed, Amadeus already lay again in deep sleep. Only his face was pale and contorted slightly by sorrow.

Christoph Eusebius, however, did not ponder over the change, but extinguished the light and sought his bed. While he was looking over his day in the night, he once more caught sight of Maruschka quite distinctly standing on the hill before the evening sun and throwing her arms up in the air longingly. At the same time, an echo of the crying animal fluttered through his memory. At this instant, he already lay in dream. — — —

In the middle of the night, he rose up horrified and looked around; for somewhere there had been a crash as if someone had hurled a stone against the wooden wall of the house or a board had broken.

His alert ear could not hear anything.

But as soon as he had lost himself in slumber, the crashing kicked off again, not always in the same way. Sometimes it sounded quite softly as if it was just a rumble in the tailor himself. It finally became too urgent for Eusebius that he stop it from distressing him any-more in bed. Scantily dressed, armed with a long ruler, he marched out to run the disturbance down. He combed every corner, into the goats' stall, even into the wood shed. In the end, he arrived back in the hall without having found anything suspicious, stood still at the stairway to Maruschka's room, raised the lantern, listened and counted the steps. There were eight of them up to where the stairs made an abrupt turn. If an intruder had a craving to go up them, it was a small leap. For eight steps and the two which lay in shadow offered no difficulty. — Why should he not climb up and convince himself that everything was in order?

Maruschka with her doubled flaw was defenceless like a caraway flower head in the field margins which anyone who wants to can knock off, and yet he, as a man, and much greater still as her master, was responsible for her safety. In addition, with this opportunity, the reasons could also be dealt with for why she had abandoned the boy and house that evening and been waving to someone from the hill.

Hesitantly he opened the lantern and blew the light out. But as soon as the tailor set his foot on the first rung to climb up, his breathing began to flutter. This ridiculous attack of fear did not let him get to the second step.

He sat down on the stairs and waited in the darkness until the cold made his knees bang together.

The tailor Mandel sat for an hour and even longer in the darkness. Finally the irrational urge left him and he found a deep sleep towards morning. The next night, the nocturnal ructions recurred and in the following night, it was not a hair better. Yes, it increased rather than decreased, and Eusebius could not make head nor tail out of what was playing such a practical joke on him all night so that he could only get a few hours rest.

To get to the bottom of the matter, of whether it was a matter of natural things, Mandel gave up his business rambling, hung his spencer in the cupboard, crept into his greasy jacket again and placed himself on a secret sentry duty in his house.

He could see clearly that a change had taken place with his housekeeper. She appeared only seldomly in the living room. With restless industry, she wandered through the shed, from the stalls into the garden, across the hallway. When she had to work away at the stove, she crept primly into the corner of the stove alcove. Her gait had become inaudible, her clutching at things without sound. The dishes steamed unawares on the table, and disappeared in an almost inexplicable way after mealtimes during which the mute woman never appeared in her place. She was never seen eating, never resting. She looked pale and ill-tempered, and sometimes Mandel caught her darting a very angry glance at him.

There are people who know how to confound us as soon as they are ready to betray us. This acting strange and affronted was apprehended by the tailor, who was well versed in all the tricks of the world, as nothing but the proof of hidden undertakings which had been begun by the mute woman against him. He saw in his imagination rope ladders tumbling out dormer windows and nocturnal visitors climbing into his housekeeper's chamber. For that reason, he doubled his vigilance. No pecking in the night escaped him. The slumbering bleats of the goats appeared to him like suppressed laughter. He heard the lock on the front door creaking gently, and when the wind skimmed over the roof, it seemed to him as if someone was creeping across the floor in stockings.

One night it tormented him even more than before. He even heard something like passionate sighing down the hallway as he stood in sudden befuddlement and devoured every noise with his ears; there, now it groans again! It did not continue. No! His teeth firmly clenched, ready for anything, the tailor climbed halfway up the stairs until his head rose above the floor of the upper storey, and he watched Maruschka's bed for a long time. He saw it there quite distinctly in the half-light of the moon which skimmed through the dormer window above it. Now he perceived exactly how restive it was becoming. The covers billowed, a bare arm stretched out and fell back floundering on the bed.

The tailor's breath faltered and his entire body shook.

"Pssst!" he voiced, and added indignantly in thought, "What is it! Will you just stop it, damned mute!" Then he repeated again his outraged "Pssst!" Then it was stock still.

The bed stood peacefully like a coffin in the loft's grey air which was becoming shimmeringly hot. The round gable window hung like a pale face above it in the darkness and stared at him with menacing horror.

Eusebius would have liked to have sent his warning "Pssst" under the roof once more, but reconsidered and climbed soundlessly down to his bed.

The next morning, he was determined, whatever the cost, to cut this wart off. Maruschka stepped, according to her habit, heedlessly and indifferently into the living room. Only Mandel did not let her fluff her way out again. He aimed his remarks at her and directed his steady, interrogating eyes at her.

But this went down nicely with her.

She not only endured his look. No, red splotches appeared in her face, she straightened up to her full height, measured him from head to toe and shook her head with dismissive laughter as if to say, "What are you thinking then?" And when, as proof of the legitimacy of his suspicions, he wanted to come to the nocturnal ructions, his tongue caught itself on a glowing thread and his arms remained firmly at his sides as if they were neatly sewn down.

With scornful laughter, the mute woman brought the scene to an end and strode to the door. But there she turned on her heel and set on the tailor again in extreme irritation.

Her face glowed. Her bust was seething as if in spasms. Her entire body was shaking. From her mouth came a bubbling, pounding and rumbling, and she was hurling her arms indignantly over everything the tailor had massed against her: he should worry about neither the goats, nor the saltbush, neither the stairs, nor the rooms, but rather stick to his trade. Every day the people would come and remind him of the delivery of orders and if he did not sit down to it, the farmer Hübner would fetch his half-finished jacket and send it to another tailor.

Christoph was speechless and looked full of astonishment at the whirl of arms which sprayed like a red fire in the air before him.

8

The tailor Mandel had come thus far through the last song of Amadeus.

His house lay on him like an incubus. Maruschka sank back after her wild flare-up entirely behind the wall of her doubled closure. His boy stole around him in wide arcs like a stranger. All the shimmer and all the dance had sunk back into the rough walls of the house and Eusebius got no further than an empty pottering and did not know in from out.

It surely stemmed from that evening upon which Amadeus, in his bed behind his father's back, had witnessed with him the strange crying of an animal, that the boy was possessed by the image of Eusebius and Maruschka hanging, caught in a red sphere, from an invisible cord high in the night. The sullen sorrow with which the mute woman was surrounded made his foster mother still more hidden to him than had been the case earlier. Yes, the boy could not explain the tailor's taciturnity in any other way than by thinking that Maruschka's muteness was lying like a wicked spell over his father and robbing him of words. For days he crept after the housekeeper to find out where she did the incantation so as to bring it to his father. But Amadeus did not discover anything other than catching her in the stalls once, standing in the corner and crying. The sounds she emitted sounded so terrible to his delicate ears that he ran away frightened.

Thus in these weeks, the child had in truth neither father nor mother. He had barely a true joy. For as soon as he was tempted to let his soul fly up into the radiance through a song, he only had to look at his father, crouched pale and stooped at the cutting table, and the ringing waves dispersed in him. For all the world, the boy would have not brought himself to sing his father into the arms of the mute woman again so that he would have to turn white and tremble like that time.

Only sometimes the lonely Amadeus would be greeted out of the clouds of the earliest part of the day by a white figure, that dream being which he had once seen vanish into the illuminated gate to heaven and which he called his mother.

The child's soul burst apart within. Around this image weaved and circled everything that was refused to him in song and from which he could not get away.

He was filled as if by intoxication and stupefaction when the stream of hidden tones was set off in him.

Then, whether he stood or sat, ran or lay, he was as if enchanted: his large eyes became still wider and shimmered, his narrow face took on the look of a great suffering. And when the magic which he heard within left him, he walked away with steps which were awkward and stumbling, his head hung to the side, and the expression on his face was extinguished, almost inane. He sat on stones, seemingly occupied by nothing, and let the sunlight stream over himself; walked in the fields lost in thoughts, humming incomprehensible things, and started with a deep breath when someone talked to him. He seemed to everybody to be a retarded dolt.

But the little wagons of life rush past men without break, and if you fall off one, the next one picks us up again. Children in particular, however, are like little birds who are always falling on their wings.

On the day which would lead Amadeus a good bit further into his dreamlike life, the farmer Hübner, splenetic over the negligence, had sent his little girl with a note to the tailor Mandel and informed him in it that the ordered jacket must be delivered on the Sunday of the Day of the Apostles at the latest, that is, in the third week of September. Otherwise he would like to keep the cloth and make a dressing gown out of it.

Little Veronika Hübner entered the Mandel house in the early afternoon. Eusebius pocketed the slap in the face with a bittersweet smile, apologised at length and in depth and promised to arrive at the farmstead in Röhrsdorf with the work certainly before the intended deadline. Then he gave the girl an uncoiled ball of yarn to play with and let her tread the secured sewing machine. He attempted to please the child in every way and delay her so his boy could yet meet her and sulk with her. By such treats, he hoped to appease the infuriated farmer again.

But Amadeus stayed away. He had already slipped outside in good time between the stubble and beet fields, in the ditches and potato furrows, not all too far from his father's house so that he could still see its chimney balanced straight on the roof ridge like a little, white cap. There he caught beetles, imprisoned them in little paper cartons, saw the diving bell spiders scurrying over the pond, collected the tiny seed capsules from the rhinanthus, and thereby went further and further towards the end of the village, taciturn and bewitched as ever.

The path on which he gradually disappeared strove gently downhill towards a rock barrier which, heavily covered with bushes, tailed off into the fields like a green wall. But before the narrow little lane, a hole drilled into the darkness, it turned in a few twists and then shot dead straight and steeply downhill.

The tailor's boy was standing at this abrupt place when Veronika decided not to wait any longer for him and cautiously slipped away. He was measuring the locality with critical looks. And even though it would have pleased him to do the same to the path and scurry down at a quick run between the cool trees, he sat down on a stone by the edge of the lane and looked raptly for a long time down at the bush wall until a magical glimmer began to float amongst the trees.

The trees were holding their crowns exhaustedly in the still heat, and Amadeus was amazed at how they could stand so motionless on their single leg without falling over. Deep in the green somewhere, a woodpecker was knocking as if with a little hammer at the wood, and the boy, who was neither familiar with nor saw the bird, thought it must be a tiny little man who was beating so loudly, and he waited for him to come forth and tell him a story, because his father no longer liked to talk with him. Perhaps he even knew the way to his mother. Not long afterwards, when he had pondered that, he heard behind himself soft, short steps and thought that what he had wished for was happening and the little knocking man was approaching him straightaway, but he could not comprehend how the little man had flown behind him so suddenly. The patter came closer and closer, and Amadeus shut his eyes in great anticipation so as not to frighten the little man. Then the little man was finally standing by him and the tailor's boy heard him breathing on him.

"Have you lost your way, boy, and don't know your way home?" a voice, beautiful like no other Amadeus had heard in his life, asked after a moment's wait.

He did not answer, however, but just shook his head so that the little miracle man would continue speaking.

But the little man also paused for a while in silence. Then soft fingers stroked his eyes and asked, "Why don't you open your eyes and look around? Are you blind?"

"No," answered Amadeus, "but if I don't look, I hear everything you say better and you can also show me the way to my mother."

"Where is your mother then?"

"Well, my father says she is in heaven. And if it is light, no path can exist. But when I make it dark around me, like in the goats' night, then a silver one can appear again and I will go up to her and be able to sing again."

The little boy said all that with a nervous, avid voice and then sat down again quite still with lowered head.

"Who are you then?" the questions continued.

"That you will already know. For aren't you the little miracle man?"

Then such a hearty laughter sounded at once that the tailor's boy opened his eyes perplexed. Only he would have liked to have closed them again, for next to him stood a girl, not buch bigger than him and not clothed much differently than the farmers' children in summertime. A flowery headscarf sat on her head, and a little, red cotton dress went down a little further than the knees on her little, bare legs. She was still laughing as if it was pouring out of her and looking amusedly at Amadeus at the same time.

"You're the tailor Mandel's boy, right?" she then asked. But Amadeus still could not talk. For if the little miracle man had not come from the forest, then the girl had been sent to him from the brightest magic of his soul so that she seemed no less wonderful and he could barely believe she had a mother and father like the other children and was of this world, and he looked at her with large, astonished eyes without turning.

Thus the girl had enough time to observe the tailor's boy of whom she had already heard all kinds of strange things among the other children, and the quiet, observant earnesty of this prematurely alert face suited his nature. For it looked as if the boy lamented constantly over having no mother.

For that reason, the little girl erupted from embarrassment into a precipitous chatter and said with many digressions that she was Veronika Hübner and had been to Amadeus's father, the tailor, so that he would finally make the jacket which had been ordered such a long time ago.

Her words sounded spry and it seemed to the boy like a little bird was singing. For that reason, he just stood and listened and wished it would never end. But in the end, Veronika had said everything that occurred to her, of the many cows in her father's stalls at their Röhrsdorf farmstead, of her white sheep which ran after her like a dog, and of the school. She did not know anything else, stooped, plucked at the grass here and there and asked Amadeus this and that. But it was as if Maruschka's muteness was crouching on him, and he barely answered with a "yes" or a "no". But when he noticed that Veronika was getting ready to go home, he grasped her hand ardently and asked if she would take him with her. Although he was determined not to cry, his voice sounded sad anyway.

The girl was somewhat taken aback by the unexpected ardour of the Mandel boy, still more admittedly by his silence and the peculiar look which pleased her more than other boys' screaming and mad springing about.

Hence she said to Amadeus that he should wait there until she returned, and ran the little bit of path back to the Mandel house. There she asked the master to let his boy go with her, and soon returned after that with a cap, for the boy was bare-headed.

Thus the two walked along the narrow pass through the rock barrier and, not long afterwards, saw Röhrsdorf's colourful patchwork of fields lying below them. The white farmyards stood in the green grass and were so large that they seemed to the tailor's boy to be ever so many towns. Between the farmsteads, ponds broadened and on each swam geese and ducks so that the water seemed littered with tiny, white ships.

Amadeus was astonished by everything and looked time and time again at Veronika from the side because he thought it all belonged to her. His emphatic eyes, full of delight in his astonishment, unlocked many a door in Veronika which she hardly knew she had, and the girl fell into genuine rambling with words the way it probably ambushes all rich people when the astonished look of the poor raises their worth into the immeasurable.

Thus they arrived at the Hübner farm and the farmer's wife was taken aback by the boy who had no mother except for the deaf-mute Maruschka and yet stood so steadily and ably before her as if an attentive heart cared for him day after day. She stroked his forehead and talked to him with kindness and love so that Amadeus felt he was with his mother in heaven. There was also thick buttered bread and milk and honey, as much as he wanted, and when the children had sated themselves, they ran through the farmyard. In the stalls, Veronika gave each cow by name. The animals turned their heads to the pair and looked at them from large, astonished eyes. All shyness and distance disappeared from Amadeus, and when they stood in front of the horses, he said his father had once ridden on one almost as far as France, and when he was grown up, then he would likewise journey to Hildesheim, Hamburg and Berlin. Veronika listened and laughed time and time again so that the life of the tailor's boy seemed to him to be as beautiful and light as before. During all the talking, they had strolled from the farmyard through the garden to the pond. There they sat and threw flowers in the water. The red of the approaching evening was already climbing. The pond lay like a shiny, great pane of glass, and the sky, with all its enraptured little clouds, was breathing its image into it, and if you wanted to see it, you only had to bend forward and look at the bottom. Then it seemed as if the entire glory of the high air was coming up through a dark gate in the earth. Veronika said it was made by the merman to lure children and draw them to him in the pond. For that reason, they ran away a distance into the meadow and hunted for the duck and goose feathers which lay scattered in the grass. Amadeus got so many that he was able to fill his pockets and could hardly hold them with both hands. Hence they let the feathers fly. Some winged away and vanished like little airships into the heights; others settled in bushes as if they wanted to be birds and build nests in the branches. The children also sang to them the little rhyme of the cockchafer and blew them away laughing. Meanwhile it was getting dark and suddenly the tailor Mandel was standing with them. He did not appear like a man, but like a gnome who falls from a tree or pops out of the earth, looking raptly at the play of the two and hesitantly giving his hat a twitch. Amadeus, who noticed what he was driving at, fled to Veronika and, before Eusebius could say anything, the little boy stated that he wanted to remain with his friend. It was only when the girl said Amadeus could let just one feather float in the wind to the Röhrsdorf farmstead and then she would come and visit him that he acquiesced. She also gave him a kiss in parting and then ran quickly into the farmyard.

The two walked into the thick twilight. The farms soon lay below them and before the path crept into the bush, Amadeus reached into his trouser pocket and let a feather fly. He was so full of the new attraction that he could find no end to the telling. But the happier the boy's words clustered together, the more monosyllabic his father became. The displaced little man strove onward, brooding to himself. His gait was more uneven than usual.

When the house under the maple emerged before them, he stopped, took his child's hand and looked around to every side to see if anyone was nearby, and then he said with aching voice, "Look, Amadeus, the bird doesn't know whether it is raising a cuckoo and what man sometimes throws away as a stone is perhaps the eye from his head." Then he walked stooped under his roof, and the child who did not understand him followed him timidly and afraid.

On that same evening, he did not wash and slept with his little hand covering his mouth so as not to lose Veronika's kiss.

The glow which Amadeus took to sleep with him was not transformed and wrested from him by his dreams. With his first step in the morning, the boy stood again in the middle of the previous day's magic. Not far from the little strip of meadow over which the twisted willow exercised its dominion, in the midst of one of the sour meadows of the farmer Schnallke, a little wilderness of hazel shrubs, bird cherries and scarlet elder proliferated and a few spindle bushes grew amongst them too. They clustered disordely and thick around a heap of field stones and had been whispering and arguing day and night since they had grown up about how they could get rid of the hindering, obtuse stones or at least cover them with their shadow. But however much they toiled, they did not raise a long enough branch to be able to bury the stones under a green roof. There was always still another funnel through which the sun poured light down undisturbed so that the mountain of stones sparkled happily with its flickering eyes. Amadeus fled to this green rotunda from the procrastination and encumbrances of the tailor's house. None of the Röhrsdorf houses could be seen, and the call of bells from the church tower at Neudeck was seldom heard sinking down from the heights. There the boy could do what he wanted and the bushes told no one else. At the top of the heap, the little boy rolled around a stone which had a depression in the middle like a comfortable seat. Then he clambered up and sat on the throne like the Kings of Prussia. The cool swirling air which lay over the roots of the bushes was warmed by the sinking heat of the sun and sashayed through the green chimneys straight up into the sky. Amadeus saw the leaves on the lowest branch moving gently as if someone was coming wandering invisibly to him. And actually, while he sat there and waited to see what would happen, a butterfly with two blue eyes on its wings whirled through the leaves. It was instantly seized by the air current and carried into the heights. The tender little creature glided so closely past the boy's face that his cheeks were stroked by the wings as though from an infinitely soft caress. At this moment, the kiss occurred to Amadeus, which Veronika had given to him the previous evening, and it seemed to him as if he had just then been touched again by the girl's lips. This brought such a joyful shock over him that he was still looking after the butterfly with bated breath when it had already been carried away through the green funnel a long time before. A play of varied colours glimmered in the place where the blue sky had absorbed it. In this flowering, Amadeus stammered raptly the name of his beloved, "Veronika! Veronika!" And when everything remained still, he added, "Come to me from your great pond. I am all alone and would like to play with you."

He said it so softly, like little children often talk to themselves when they are alone so that nobody hears but their own avid little soul which bears these words.

But Veronika Hübner made no reply from the Röhrsdorf farmstead to her little friend's call, even though he listened into the heavens for a long time from his little dream room.

Only, a black bird came zooming down in the end and settled on the highest tip of the bushes. It inflated its feathers, held its head askew and looked down at the boy. Then it flew away with a clapping sound.

Then Amadeus recalled the words the girl had spoken to him in parting the day before: if he wanted her to come and visit him, then he must let a feather go in the wind. And he reached into his pocket and set free one of the feathers which he had brought with him from the Hübner's pond. To begin with, this feather did not want to fly, but tumbled and would have liked best of all to creep among the roots of the bushes. But the boy helped it with his hand and breath until the little white airship caught the right draught. It climbed up over the branches into the air, perched on the wind and sailed forth.

Now the Mandel boy was rescued from his loneliness in a fortunate way. Every day he spent many hours in his little bushy room, diligently sent messages into the air and waited for an answer. Then it sometimes occurred that somewhere in the fields a child raised its voice and called for its mother or siblings. And when such a call was carried a good distance and sounded quite beautiful, Amadeus thought every time that Veronika had spoken to him through the air, composed her answer with discretion and was happy beyond all measure. His little green room then expanded: meadows spread out around him, sunny fields, large, shiny ponds, all that he had seen at the Röhrsdorf farmstead, and the girl was also there with her flying little skirt and her spry bird's voice. He roamed about with his friend in his little dream garden and told her everything that passed over his soul.

When the pond feathers had all gone, he collected together others and sent them as messengers on the same path. But so that they, not yet knowing Veronika, would find their way to the Hübner farm, he gave away something special to them each time. He imitated the girl's beautiful chatter so that they would know who it was amongst the children that he meant. And because Amadeus did not incorporate into words everything which he had in his heart for his playmate, he stretched them and filled the verve and ungovernable sound of his soul into them.

In this way, Amadeus returned to his singing, and since his father was not there, he dared to sing louder and louder. Not long afterwards, he also sent a feather airship to the motherly farmer's wife, even to the farmer whom he did not know. The sound of the basin of patch-work fields was in his song, the sound of the pond chuckling against its banks, and the high flight of little red clouds.

People passing not far away on the path to Sauerborn or to Ranser and the mountain cottages were surprised by it, crept up for that reason and bent the branches apart to see the singer. But when they recognised the Mandel boy, they were seduced into talk against Christoph Eusebius which he would not have tucked behind the mirror if it had been written down.

9

The new singing play of his boy did not admittedly remain hidden from the tailor. In a memory which the master could not raise clearly, he knew the boy and his songs had actually been driven into the fields by him. But he did not admit this to himself. Clandestinely he reached the general conviction that he must have sent Amadeus out with his singing because he was disturbing his work. Around the last dream kiln of his soul, furthermore, the whiff was sometimes given off of an idea that, even from a distance, his boy's song was not having a favourable influence on him. Then he crept around his little boy's fabled space and listened to all the forms of his singing: of the hole in the water, the little knocking man, the farmer's wife Hübner and her husband. Most frequently he heard Amadeus singing about Veronika, the little girl. Of him and Maruschka, he sang only ever the stupid, completely distorted song of the red sphere. For that reason, the hidden scourge pricked the master more than once to such an extent that he was already bending the branches to chase the boy from his hidden throne of fancies. Only a soft, sweet thing, an inconceivable beauty which old Mandel only lived through the little boy's voice hindered him from it. He always got a hold of himself in the nick of time and returned to his house without having touched his child.

But when he sat again at his cutting table and the soft echo of Amadeus's voice skimmed through the open window past his ear, it often became hot and narrow in the pit of his heart so that he almost had to scream.

In the nights which followed such days, the rumbling in the house also kicked off anew. Christoph Eusebius had no bodily peace and kept watch for hours again on the stairs.

During these confused visitations, the tailor worked incessantly on Hübner's jacket. On a long, sleepless night, it was finally finished. With the grey of dawn, he sewed the last button on. He hung it on the wall and laid himself down to sleep. In the bright morning, he awoke, completely disordered and exhausted, with the feeling of having reached the end of a long, gruelling journey. The room lay soundless in a turgid light, quite without life.

Amadeus had plunged outside again already into the bushes, and he could hear Maruschka washing the wooden dishes in the pool under the willow. He propped his head on his elbows and followed with un-thinking ears the lapping of the water and the banging together of the dishes. At the same time, his soul was creeping halfway back to sleep. He lay and blinked with his wrinkled little eyes. Without knowing what he said, he continuously asked himself softly, "What shall it be then? That is no harvest? You, Christoph, hey, what is it then?"

A strand of grey hair fell across his forehead, was stroked away by him again, but kept sinking again over his eyes.

Suddenly he lay in a pitch black cloud, his chest was clenched by such a fear that he was unable to breath. As he recovered from this attack as if from a dull blow, the certainty stood starkly before his eyes that he was sit-ting backwards on the horse and if he did not pull himself together, like in the butcher's yard halfway to Hamburg where he sprung over the two or three metre high wall in front of two policemen, it would seize him by the collar and squeeze the vapour from him. In this way, as he was driving it now, it must not continue; oth-erwise it would consume his house and himself.

As if kicked, he sprung up and got dressed. While walking about, he buttoned his vest. From the field, a metallic tinkling rang out slowly, the sharpening of a scythe by an indolent reaper. With each tone, the tailor's fingers shoved a button through the buttonhole. At the same time, he counted, "One ... two ... three ...", up to eight. Strange. When his vest was buttoned, the tinkling outside stopped. Eusebius paused and wondered over this coincidence.

Then it shot through his head: eight, exactly eight weeks, his life had waded through this turbid, sluggish dawdling. Spying for deliverance, his eyes searched the walls of his living room. He noticed the Hübner jacket hanging on the hook and felt consolingly tapped on the shoulder that the time had not been entirely needlessly thrown away. And now a different wind would go through his maple, one without effort.

If he hurried, he would still get down to the Röhrsdorf farmsteads before midday and could deliver the jacket to the Hübner farm.

He drew his coffee can out from the stovepipes and set about his breakfast. Between chewing and swallowing, he worked out the bill, item after item, stiff canvas, lining, silk and so on, and put on a tenner or a little more so that the farmer had something to haggle down.

Then he took his Sunday coat from the cupboard, spread it out on the bench and lay the bamboo stick over it. But before he slapped the jacket into the oilcloth, he undertook a precise inspection of whether the tacking had all been removed and whether it was in a state to pass before critical looks. He plucked here and there, flicked with his fingers, spread it out before him, held it at arm's length, hung it on the hook again and took a step back. For some work is only correctly appreciated from a distance. But he did not like to stand to the left or the right, allow the sun entrance or let the shadows play on it: no lighting, no distance helped. The jacket had simply not worked out. This work, which in its main ideas had seemed so perfectly thought out and tailored, had suffered under the nightwatches, the rumblings, the emotional unrest, the rushed heat and all the confused visitations as though under an uninterrupted rebellion and to such an extent that it actually looked, if he was honest, merely like a great patchwork of rags whose joining together formed a sack, open at bottom and top, on which the arms hung quite absurdly like two sinuous bags and the seams crept around disorderly like knobbly worms in every part of this disastrous piece of clothing. Nothing in it pointed to the timid attempt to fit it to the body of a real farmer.

When Mandel had convinced himself of the pointlessness of any attempt at alteration, cold sweat appeared on his forehead. He placed the jacket on the bench next to his coat, sank with crossed arms over it and it would not have taken much for him to break into tears.

It was not a derailment of his over abundant spirit. From this confusion of every principle, no trace led to a gentler existence, let alone a path to the courts of the rich and noble, as he had thought in the beginning. His meditations threw him down a black shaft and let him fall down as though onto pitiless stones so that it swirled around him like sparks being thrown up. Outside Maruschka was still rattling the wooden dishes in the pool under the willow. The tailor wanted to think just then that it would be really all the same to him if he was not a master but a grain of oat, then everyone's best hen could devour him and it would put an end to his entire little bit of life in the simplest way. But he could not spin out this idea. The mute woman was pumping the jugs constantly against each other. From the bushes, his boy's voice was winging its way now and rejoicing over this dull, crude drumming sound in the summer light.

And while Mandel was forced to listen to this music, shrunken, broken over his botched life, his despair transformed into wild rage. Had it really been the mute woman alone who had driven him for weeks through confused days and disturbed nights and finally thrust him here over the bench?! Heedlessly, indifferently, without any sympathy! And now she had succeeded in breaking him, she was performing this mocking drumming outside.

With closed eyes, he saw her bust inflate, her full arms reddening, her entire, welling body rocking and turning with pleasure. Then the deathly sore tailor was pulled upright. His eyes were wide with longing and flickered like the eyes of a forest creature mad with thirst. He sprang to the window and threw a devouring glance at her, but rebounded. For just then the mute woman had straightened up and turned her face to him, still red from stooping, in which an obscured smile lay.

Now he could hear her coming up to the house.

If she now entered the room, the tailor felt, he would then have to lunge at her and there would be a misfortune. To guard against that and protect himself and his boy from disgrace, he bolted the door and braced himself against it to prevent his housekeeper from entering.

But the mute woman strolled past the front door and disappeared into the vegetable garden behind the shed. Then the afflicted Eusebius had just enough sense to quickly throw his coat on, grasp his stick and leave the house in flight.

He went in a great arc around the bushes from which Amadeus's voice rang out now and then, and turned behind the Moser tavern onto the Schrimsteig path. Without looking around, he hurried at a breathless pace into the forest which stretched to the frontier, as if he were determined to leave his life behind and emigrate from the Kingdom of Prussia never to be seen again.

Around midday the mute woman stepped into the living room and saw the master's clothing lying strewn disorderly on the floor.

She was frightened and paled all over, but after short consideration, lit the fire in the stove, placed the soup on it and took the plates from the pot cupboard, in short, she applied herself calmly to her duties as if the tailor would enter at any moment.

The hand of the clock moved over to twelve, and Mandel was not to be seen.

Maruschka pulled the soup pot out of the embers and began the search. She looked out every window, walked through the entire house, and when she returned empty-handed again to the living room, she gathered up the master's clothes, took them in her arms, brushed them down carefully and hung them in the cupboard. At the same time, she bent forward too far, lost her balance a little and, in seconds, had fallen between her master's things, bouncing back into the room with swaying glances. She narrowed her eyes and shook herself with an irate smile. Then she went and looked for Amadeus. But while she was standing and looking out, a gurgling unexpectedly full of anguish erupted in her. In the end, it became so violent that she had to go into the wood shed until it was over.

Eusebius was meanwhile running around aimlessly in the forest. He was upset, that was clear. His life's belongings lay strewn confusedly around him. Only with clarity and decisiveness could something then be done. But his mind was like that of someone who wants to eat soup with a fork, for hardly had his mastery hitched itself somewhere than his fury over Maruschka intervened and everything boiled in hot steam. It was goading him again like in the weeks before, and in the evening, he had achieved nothing but seeing his house lying before him in the darkness and looking at it full of anguished expectation.

"Either me or her", he finally said to himself, stuck his stick between the leaves on the soft forest floor and hung his hat on the hook. That's right, her! He had to begin with that. For the confusion emanated from nothing else but her self-will. She did what pleased her, roamed about and took away everything he had with those averted eyes, that mocking smile, that unbearable shrug of the shoulders.

"I'll put her in harness, but not too tightly", he thought, rising up more and more. "I was not frightened before that Napoleon, so I will be able to put a woman's head right."

Half an hour later, he was again sitting at his cutting table with the irrevocably fixed intention of leading his housekeeper back under his old dominion and showing proper mastery over her.

The mute woman was astonished to see the master so abruptly in his usual place. Mandel acted as if she were not present and pursued her inconspicuously with the smouldering of his plan. When she bent down, he thought, 'Yes, just bend over! I have made the farmer Franzel a coat like no other in the surrounding area. I will deal with you too.'

When she straightened up and stepped stoutly across the room, he seethed within, 'the tall joker is a fellow like a tree and — wears trousers from my own hand.' No, no! Eusebius was not frightened.

The deeper it passed into evening, the fiercer and more reckless he became, the more consuming his glances lay around him. Everything around him was growing: the walls like high ramparts; the light of the little table lamp blazed like a red, jittery fire; the tolling of the hour sounded like the pounding of a great hammer, and the swing of the pendulum seemed to him to be soundless, portentous strokes of a scythe. He sat and turned the cloth with trembling hands; he sewed and did not know to where he was sewing, waxed the cotton without having threaded it.

At the same time, he followed everything with timid stealth and cheered himself in silence, 'Just wait, right, right!'

Now Amadeus finally undressed, knelt in the little bed and prayed, called his sheepish "good night" across and, after a few soft sighs, swam with gentle breaths towards his dream.

Now Maruschka was also finished with the washing up, shaking out the wrung wash cloth and hanging it on the oven door to dry. After that she stepped to the pot cupboard, sought out the key to the wood shed and left the room.

Now Mandel had to act. The front door fell shut. The sound acted on the tailor like a kick in the chest. With pounding heart and shaking knees, he got up. He was walking like a stiff ladder. But he tore the door open and drilled his eyes with such a boldness into the darkness of the meadow that the darkness crept into the corners like a beaten up, black cat.

"Yes, yes", the tailor said to himself, "I am Christoph Eusebius Mandel! There is nothing more to it."

With these encouraging words, he stepped into the open, drew the door shut behind him and pressed himself into a corner. He wanted to have the matter with Maruschka fought out there in the meadow, for a child should know nothing of its parents' arguments.

The latch to the goats' stall was still open. He pushed it in again. But it did not catch. The goats were becoming restive and bleating.

"Be quiet, you devil", he breathed in excitement.

Then steps were shuffling through the grass.

He quickly tore the padlock off and stuck it in his pocket.

He still had time to take a step to the side, then the door opened.

The tailor's teeth began to chatter. Convulsively, he thought, 'I have ... the tall joker is wearing my trousers ... I have ... I have ... I have ...'

Maruschka had entered and was groping for the door handle.

Now her full shoulder skimmed him. Suddenly the tailor felt it turning like a whirlwind. The meadow flickered. A great, hot door was opening.

Snivelling, Christoph Eusebius staggered into it. At the same time, he stuttered continuously, "The tall joker is wearing my trousers ... The tall joker is wearing my trousers ..."

Soft and warm, the mute woman closed her arms around him. The strange, bestial cry, but now jerking as though in inexpressible ardency, rang out again. Mandel absorbed it like the seething hum with which midsummer strolls across ripe ears of corn.

Talali, talali, talali-i-i-, his boy's song intoned around him.

In strong arms, more carried than walking, he floated up the eight steps of the loft stairs up to where they made the sharp turn and then continued on up.

10

After this successful night, everything in the Mandel house turned itself again towards the old tracks. A few days later, Christoph Eusebius had delivered a pair of trousers to the farmstead of the farmer Tautz in Ranser. At another time, it would have taken the master's breath away a little to transact business with the man. For he was a fellow, crudely put together like a cow trough, the biggest lout on the Ranser mountain, and that says something in a place where the men hew their opinions with whips about the ears. Tautz was numbered in general among the crooked sheriffs and that was his grudge. For all of his gaunt, tall body was in order up to his belly. There, as a sort of bulbous buoy, was a sort of giant gall nut, not over the middle of the crotch, but further off, a little over the left trouser pocket.

The master thought his work to be his best and raked with his bamboo stick playfully in the soft path during his walk, in the manner of that sort of young fellow who is constantly itched by high spirits. When the tailor now entered the farmer's living room, the latter was just calling his wife names because she was tolerating the neighbour's hens in his garden, and swore not to leave a bone in the body of the feather duster if it happened again. Then he grasped the trousers from the oilcloth, looked down, inspected them, and vanished into the next room. His wife, however, sat down by the master and attempted a friendly conversation, for she had a tender, quiet nature and sought to blot out the bad impression her husband's rumbling had left behind. But when a pair of boots flew against the wall inside, she rose and went out. Mandel counted the panes in the windows and smiled. Just as he got to the last one, the door flew open and Tautz came out in a rage and placed himself with his legs apart in front of Eusebius. "Twenty four", Mandel said and did not realise that he was speaking aloud.

"No, a hundred", the farmer roared, "a hundred times you are not clever, tailor."

"Why are you shouting so? If roaring was cleverness then oxen would stand at every pulpit instead of pastors", Mandel answered with the friendliest demeanour in all the world.

At this unexpectedly sharp reply, Tautz became somewhat more amiable, and because nobody else was in the room before whom he could make himself ridiculous with pandering, the farmer said quite politely that the trousers were quite good in most respects, but did not sit right around the belly.

Eusebius noted straightaway that he had arched the trousers on the other side of the belly to that which the farmer's body admitted, that is, on the right instead of the left side, but shook his head, made a very aggrieved face and finally said it was all absolutely correct as it should be, but Tautz must be ill. For when he had taken his measures, his belly had been on the right side. Only, such things, and sometimes even worse, just happened in the world. There were kidneys that wandered; why could a belly not shift too? There he would have to talk to a doctor. But if he placed no little value on the experience of a much-travelled man, then he advised him to fasten a sealing wax plaster on the diseased part and let it lie there as long as it takes to fall off by itself again. That was cheap and would return the old ease and firmness to his body. Of course, he must abstain during this time from all agitation and excitement. For nothing harms such inner suffering more than anger and shouting. After that he looked the crooked sheriff in the eye and implied to him that it was really not right in his belly, for it had a quince yellow skin covering. Christoph Eusebius said all that with calm conviction so that the farmer began to be a bit distraught.

Only the tailor had for too long had no fun and had thus been weaned off the pleasure somewhat. Hence, when he saw the wrinkled brow of the crooked sheriff, he could not hold back a smile. Then Tautz noticed that Mandel had just treated him with scorn, walked calmly into the next room and did not appear again for a long time. His face was pale with fury. He threw the trousers onto the table so that the buttons rattled and screamed, "I'm not taking the trousers! Drop your stupidity, and if you don't find your way quickly out of the yard, I'll set the dogs on you." Under these circumstances, the tailor was quickly outside. But when he was descending the mountain, just then the sun came out. He saw his house lying under the maple and looking up at him with gleaming windows.

Then it came over him. He stepped behind a bush and made a little skip of joy.

On the way, he had to go to the Upper Röhrsdorf tavern, past the Moser tavern, which lay behind an ancient lime tree a few steps from the road. There three men were standing before the door, waving their hands about, arguing with each other and then laughing loudly. When they caught sight of the tailor, they called out to him that he was arriving on time. Such a one as Mandel, they would not have needed, for when he arrived, there were at once fifteen more there. So as not to provoke their mockery, he went and sat with them at the table. The men's chatter swung back and forth amusingly, and the master, to whom it seemed as if he had come under a new sun, gave as good as he got, and when someone had dug a hole for him, then he played the grown-up fool as a reward. Finally the most serious of them said that was enough with the mucking about, now they must continue with the sheriff's election. That very winter, namely, the change in the council leadership would take place. According to old custom, the Upper Röhrsdorf residents opened this business, which always brought a violent commotion into the cottages and farmsteads, with a satirical poem. The three men were now about to fulfill the post of election bards and hang a dry slur on each of the most probable candidates. They squeezed their sprays of vinegar towards Sauerborn, and read aloud what they had achieved.

> If I were the miller of Sauerborn,
> Then every day I'd get a horn;
> For while I'm milling in the wheel house,
> My wife is beating the sacks out.

Eusebius then told them about the fun he had with the farmer Tautz, showed the trousers around and acted the entire scene out with such fitting merriment that the three almost fell out of their seats with laughter.

Then he sat to the side and made up a little verse over the crooked sheriff. After he had finished, he presented the slip of paper to the three with the stipulation that they not betray him, the poet, and vanished while they were reading it.

The lines read,

> If I were Tautz over the valley,
> I'd stick a gnome in my belly.
> He'd creep sometimes left, sometimes right,
> That'd make my belly tight.

They ran out and called after the tailor, laughing. But he just waved from a distance with his cap and strove onwards to his house.

So Eusebius was again entering into the blessings of his thousand disordered transformations. The dreams cleared from the rough walls and filled the Mandel house with their invisible, colourful vapour; the windows sucked in the light of the sparse autumn sun and breathed it over the master's diligent hands.

That he sometimes climbed up to the loft with Maruschka and was allowed to look through the colourful panes also gave Eusebius no small pleasure. And as all human desire is most undimmed when nobody knows anything of it, the tailor liked these views into the surrounding area where Adam and Eve were spinning their little dance, quite uncurtailed because of the pleasures which he lost himself in with the mute woman, and which nothing disturbing in his day could reverberate against. Nothing wrong hung about him. Yes, he considered his entire life to be a single exalted success. It went for him like the wanderer who at the end of his journey gilds every adversity and sees all disappointments as fruitions. He had not ruined Hübner's jacket, instead he had delivered it a dozen times under ever new circumstances as finished work. The ineffectual patrolling during the confused weeks appeared to him to be like a single triumphal procession of his masterly skillfulness. He was fought for. He saw in his memory the farmers wives asking endearingly for his craftsman's services and heard himself being called by all the men in the fields. And all the secrets which he had learnt from his life, all the wonders he had enjoyed, lay well preserved in the twofold night of this woman who did not tear apart his dream wandering with words but could be sculpted by the master's imagination according to his discretion. Without his knowing it, his Amadeus's vision had come true for him, he really was hanging in a red sphere over the earth, to which he alone knew the way.

Thus Eusebius thought at least for a long time. But one day he realised that it was an illusion.

Usually the tailor only crept at night to the mute woman. This afternoon Maruschka had to work at the oven. She opened the little door and the glow of the fire ran up her arm to her bare neck and flickered in her face. To the tailor, she seemed as beautiful as he could not have held possible, and although his boy was in the room and playing, he waved to her furtively until she lay down the piece of wood and went out. After a proper interval, Mandel also put his work to the side and followed her. Whilst climbing up the stairs, a ringing sounded in his head which sounded like the voice of Amadeus. The tailor mistook it for the sounds of great desire in his ears and continued. On reentering the living room, however, his boy was looking at him with timidly searching eyes. The toy had slipped from his hand. He sat fearfully and did not dare stir.

Eusebius was hit with strange depth by Amadeus's look, so that he had to look out the window. From now on, he observed more precisely and realised that Amadeus was taking part in his hidden undertakings through his song: whenever he crept up to lie with Maruschka, the most muffled of steps rang themselves in the rhythm of the childlike voice; in the shingles and rafters, his song swished in mysterious ways and once even, when Mandel was lying under a happy dominion and looking at the wall in cosy weakness, he saw on the old grey background of the wooden boards, as though from a hazy expanse, the image of his dead wife emerging, looking at him with reproachful sorrow and vanishing.

Whenever that happened to the tailor, the colourful panes through which he saw his life broke. The secret happiness crumbled, and it seemed to him as if he had only wandered through the confused, difficult weeks to sit on a little heap of rubbish in a lightless barrel.

The mute woman carried on her behaviour untouched, laughed in quiet merriment, and blossomed from one day to the next. Everything which beset him had no hold on her. Then old Mandel decided to do the same as her and make himself deaf with violence. Only he did not like so much to close himself off and not pay any mind to the boy, he was absorbing Amadeus's voice with the pores of his body against his will as it were, and heard it then ringing out from the most hidden depths of his soul as the warning of his conscience.

Sometimes, while he was observing the boy inconspicuously in order to bring out what was in him that gave his song this mysterious power to mingle in the depths of his life, Amadeus did not appear to him as a child, let alone a six year old. He was taller and leaner than all the like-aged children in the village. His movements were considered. In his gait there was something like a preacher's dignity. In his moments of quietest wistfulness, shadows sprung up in his face, as they only fall over the features of men from the spaces of anguished experience, and a fire emerged in his eyes from within so that they no longer shone blue but almost black.

Amadeus's transformation often acted so strongly on his father that he did not appear to him as his real child, but as a stranger who had broken into the house and was threatening his peace and security.

He set off at the boy as soon as he prepared to sing, yes, he did not tolerate even Amadeus writing his songs on strips of paper and letting them fly in his inner being with mute swaying and careworn face.

"Leave the flecks alone", Mandel growled, "you will undo yourself inside with the fuss and you will become nothing more than a Boniface Windel, an organ grinder."

But what could a wind start which the Lord has called into life over all the mountains of the earth? It can do nothing but skim over the treetops, and the boy hid himself deeper in his ringing insights and became all the more devotedly bound together with them.

In this new hardship, the master's gift came to his aid in turning his life and the events and visitations which he had experienced from the start of the Russian narrative into a many coloured cloth, his guileful spirit coalesced and the narrative joined his world travels as a new adventure.

That was no small work. He guided swings of the needle which looked like a lunging to strike with a stick; let the thread ring like a plucked string and skipped with stitches through the cloth like a continuous trilling.

When old Mandel thus turned his life into fable, Amadeus had to leave the room and he heard him speaking excitedly from the hallway as if he were arguing with a hostile stranger. When the child, overwhelmed by curiosity, slipped through the door to see who was there, his father sat all alone with reddened face before his work, shook his head with astonished laughter or sprung excitedly from the cutting table.

Finally Mandel was finished with the narrative, and when he thought it over once more, he realised that it had been given to him as it were by his good spirit. For he only needed to alter the denouement a little and Amadeus would have to cease that bad habit of twisting his head.

It was a bright winter's day. The sky climbed up from the silvery forest of the long bush into a pallid blue. No breeze stirred and the snow flakes fell sporadically like little, shimmering white flames in front of the Mandel house.

Then Eusebius placed the little footstool in front of him in the middle of the room and called Amadeus to take a seat on it.

The boy followed the command with apprehensiveness, for Mandel had barely climbed up to the cutting table and he was drawing his brows deep over his eyes and looking darkly at a knot in the floorboards like a pastor does when he is about to begin a sermon and has forgotten the text. Finally he breathed out, brushed his grey strand of hair into place and began with a somewhat uncertain voice, "You see, boy, I talk and preach that you should leave off with the singing and eternal piping. But you go and do otherwise, creeping into the woodshed and scribbling on paper until your hands are blue with cold, or you put yourself in with the goats and sing them something. No, no, my dear boy, I know everything."

Amadeus turned red and looked embarrassed at the dance of snowflakes out the window.

"Are you not happy with me?" the tailor asked, bitter over the child's indifference.

Amadeus lowered his head and could barely speak for the choking in his voice.

"Say now Kolivansky, Ko—li—vans—ky."

"Moli..."

"Oh, Moli ... Koli ... Kolivansky. Look, now I will tell you the story so that you know it. The singing hurts me, it makes me sick."

In the boy's face, that fear arose with which he had seen his father's need when he had sung him into Maruschka's arms the first time.

With satisfaction Christoph perceived the impression of his introductory words and continued, "Yes, yes. When I think about it today, I would soon have died as a result of Kolivansky. Well, then just listen how it was with me.

97

I had not long been a master in Upper Röhrsdorf. It had probably been ten or fifteen years. You weren't yet born. People ran to my house because nobody in the entire surrounding area wanted to be clothed by anyone but the tailor Mandel. I worked twelve hours a day and often remained awake until morning came around again. But it was no use, the cloth did not diminish from the shelf on the wall. Then I well realised that it could not remain like that and if I did not want to put my health up for sale then I had to look around for a journeyman. But it was a hard winter at the time, the roads were packed with snow that a horse could hardly get through, let alone a man, and the window panes had a pelt like a sheep before shearing.

So I waited a long time in vain for a wandering tailor fellow.

Then one afternoon a fellow stood before me unexpectedly, lean as a rifle and black as someone who'd crept out of the devil's pocket. Without knocking, he stood before me, said in broken German the craftsman's greeting, and talked about work. I asked for his name. 'Kolivansky', he answered. And before I could say yes or no, the uncanny fellow sat down next to me, threw one leg over the other and asked to sew. At first I pulled his leg gently and let him have a sniff from afar that I would rather see him with his stick on the road again. My new journeyman acted as if he suddenly did not understand German, struck his palm against his leg and cried, 'Hodne!' I did not know at the time that it meant 'quick', thinking he meant hup, became annoyed and answered that it was all the same to me whether he went hup or whoa. The main thing was that he closed the door from without.

Hardly had I blown that under his nose, than a laugh arose in Kolivansky as if he was rattling sabres in his mouth, and his eyes floated in his head like musket balls.

Then my thread of patience also tore, and I put the thumb to his Adam's apple with a few choice words.

Now Kolivansky saw with whom he had to deal and that I knew means and ways of pounding on a door which could swallow him up from one moment to the next like the cat swallows the mouse. That's why he relented and pulled out of his blue coat his apprentice's diploma and everything which a true craftsman must have on paper. He originated from Solowitz, deep in Russia, where the children are still reared on wolf's milk, and he had apprenticed in Moscow. His passport was from the Russian emperor and undersigned by Mr Gufernement.

Now I have already said that all the same an order hung from every shingle of my roof and my two hands would have had to sew with twenty needles at once to accomplish everything. Even if Kolivansky did not please me, I considered, however, that you could easily be a Russian and a reputable tailor at the same time. But, as a precaution, I said he had to first provide me with evidence of his skillfulness before I could hire him, and if he provided the sample to my satisfaction then I would keep him until the Easter lamb was slaughtered and perhaps even longer. After that I handed him material and had him make a pair of trousers, nice and roomy in the backside, spry in the knees and beautifully flared in the calves. The measurements would be in my book. Meanwhile it had become evening and Kolivansky thought he couldn't start anything that day, for he was tired and had a murderous hunger. In the morning, he would set to on the trousers and I would get the shock of my life. With that we sat down at the laid table. The Russian tailor hewed into the food as if he had the hunger of ten Cossacks complete with their horses, and did not stop before bread, potatoes, butter and cheese, in short, everything that was on the table had wandered into his belly, and hardly as much was left for the rest of us as our teeth could bite into. After he had belched, he stabbed his knife into the table top, stood up and lay down in the loft where his bed had been erected.

He snored the whole night so that it sometimes seemed as if a wooden wagon were travelling through the house, at other times as if an animal were whimpering and not a man. In between he was always banging as if someone was throwing stones at the wall.

The next morning, he again sank the bread behind his belt and then set about his work. He was accustomed to cutting according to the Odessa style, he said, and if something should at first seem odd to me, he asked me for the sake of the Black Madonna of Częstochowa to say no word of criticism, for he was hot tempered and could not for his life bear objections.

To begin with, everything went as it should. His hands were sure, and the pieces flew just so from the cloth. For that reason, I left him to do it and hardly looked at him anymore. Kolivansky himself became more and more cheerful in his work and in the end, he even began singing.

You must know, boy, Russians sing like the angels in heaven and as long as I had lived, I had not been blessed to hear a Russian song. But Kolivansky was a master at singing. What am I saying? A magician, and hardly had he opened his mouth than I seemed to be in another world. The room widened. It seemed to me as if all sorts of people were coming in and out. In front of the windows, a strange city grew with chimneys, flag poles and towers, and I did not know in my soul anymore whether I was in Röhrsdorf or Moscow.

Thus Kolivansky conducted a magnificent music making for three days. I went around as though in a dream and still don't know today what I did all that time …"

Eusebius had to break off his story here; for Amadeus, who was now sitting on the floor next to the footstool in the middle of the room, had sunk down slowly during the last sentences and was lying with his face on the floor.

"What's this all about, boy?" Mandel asked. "Are you not well?"

Amadeus shook his head.

"Shall I not continue telling?" Mandel asked again. Only the boy did not seem to hear the question. A tremor ran through his body as if it were the surface of a pond trembling under an approaching storm. The tailor thought he had received an affirmative gesture and so continued speaking, "All my bread wandered from the pantry into Kolivansky's stomach, and my senses seem to have gone through the window and to all four winds. Finally his his song broke off and in my house, it was as quiet as a crypt …"

With these words, Amadeus jumped up as though thrown and settled unnaturally erect on his legs. No muscle in his body stirred, no fibre in his face twitched. Only the pupils of his wide open eyes jittered as if seeking a foothold somewhere.

Eusebius thought the child had been frightened all too much by the wild Russian.

For that reason, he said reassuringly, "No, no, Amadeus, calm down. Kolivansky was not at all black. Well! He wasn't talll either. Amadeus!! He was quite small. Boy, just listen!"

Suddenly the boy bowed like a switch which the storm is bending, and sank soundlessly back to the floor.

With one leap, Mandel sprang from the cutting table and stood by his boy.

"What's wrong?" he stuttered.

But barely had he touched the child than the spasm dissipated and Amadeus broke out into a frantic weeping. At the same time, he wailed incessantly, "Oh father ... oh father ... oh father ..."

The tailor ran helplessly from the room, stormed through the house and called for Maruschka. He found her in the stalls and led her in gesticulating. The mute woman observed the child, shook her head smiling and bent down to lift him up. When Amadeus felt her hands on his body, he gestured like mad, struggled in mortal fear with his hands and feet against her and screamed, "Go away, go away! I want to go to Veronika!" But the tall woman gathered the whimpering boy up like a bundle and carried him to his bed.

There he continued crying until he was completely exhausted. The two stood next to him and had no idea what had thrown the gentle boy into this truculence. Finally his body lay calmly like a wilted leaf.

Eusebius went from his boy's bed with a displeasure which, it is true, he thrust on the child, but which climbed from the peculiar depths of his own life and increased the more he denied responsibility. In hours it had already turned into a fury and anger without any real direction. His lips shook, his eyeballs raced back and forth sharp and winking behind the folds of his eyelids, and he snapped wildly in the air with his long scissors the way angry beetles hack about indiscriminately with their nippers.

But Amadeus lay pale and silent, turned his back to the room and all its life, and looked with firmly clenched mouth and despairing, large eyes at the wall. He desired neither food, nor play, and it seemed as if a hidden illness was reaching for his life. His secretive anguish, his silent, seemingly defiant turning away afflicted the master harder and harder.

On the second day towards evening, the boy turned around soundlessly, and after he had watched his father's work unnoticed, he peered into the sullen passing of the light. His face seemed altered and bore the features of that hopeless, fervent anguish as buries itself in the cheeks and the forehead of ten year olds when there quixotic intentions are shattered by life for the first time. And then he rose up cautiously onto his knees and waited with a wistful pleading in his eyes for his father to look up and notice his waiting. At the same time, his mouth twitched with words for which he could not find any courage.

"Father", he finally said and lowered his glance. Eusebius surely heard the call and sensed how the child's soul approached him. But to extend his authority as an 'example', he threw scraps of cloth around twice as furiously as if he were deaf with rage.

"Father", Amadeus repeated his request still quieter and more timidly.

Then the master let his scissors fall clattering on the bench, adjusted the tape measure on his shoulders and said gruffly, "Well, have you finally bucked up, boy, and do you want to be well-behaved again?"

Amadeus lowered his head still deeper in silence and smiled painfully.

"What? Hey? Do you think perhaps that such a plonking down is nice, such a kicking and screaming, eh?"

And while old Mandel was saying this, the mute woman could be heard in the hallway preparing to enter. Then his excitement rose still higher, and the flood of the harangue swelled up and did not want to end. But Amadeus did not lift his head. His eyes remained dry and his face pale. Even when Maruschka entered and placed herself next to the passionately gesticulating master as if helping, the boy did not shake a bone and waited in calm humility.

In the end, the tailor had emptied out everything in ungovernable words and demanded that his boy ask him and Maruschka for forgiveness.

The child hesitated, then lifted his head, looked past the mute woman to his father and asked, "Would you really have to die if I sung once more?"

Mandel was not at all prepared for this question and hence asked back, "What do you mean?"

The boy choked, his lips trembled; but he could not speak.

But meanwhile the master had understood. "Yes, whether I would have to die?" he asked once more.

Amadeus nodded and looked with desperate attentiveness at his father's mouth.

"Yes, that's right", Mandel answered and fell into an ever increasing fervour. "Yes, if you had not thrown yourself down, you would have heard. I lost my senses from Kolivansky's singing. I was not successful in my work anymore, not once could I make trousers, let alone a jacket. People spurned me and in the end, I fell from pure fear down a steep, wet path in the forest, and if people had not been walking past there luckily, I would perhaps still be lying there today."

"And Moli ... Moli ...?" Amadeus asked deathly pale.

"Kolivansky. What became of him? The devil fetched him. One morning his bed was empty, and in the air all around Upper Röhrsdorf it was grey as if a great puffball had been burst. There you know now. Leave off with your piping. People just laugh at you and it makes no sense anyway. You will be a schoolboy now and have other things to do. — Well, and now come and give me a kiss and your mother too, and everything will be right again."

"He stepped up to the bed and the child lay a limp, cold kiss on Maruschka's lips. Then he sank with a soft sound of despondent anguish into the pillows again.

Because Maruschka was standing nearby, old Mandel heard nothing and climbed again into his tailor's enclosure.

11

Amadeus spent many days in bed after the story of Kolivansky.

It seemed as if he were suffering from the aftermath of a difficult illness, he lay so weakly, as if transported beyond all the mountains. When he needed to get up, he was overcome with trembling. He looked around helplessly and finally broke out into a high-pitched, powerless crying.

But Eusebius left the clapper in the bell which he had sounded; for he recalled the dying brother of his wife, who had, solely by playing music, gone from a good farm to a shed and from there into the ditch. So the tailor transformed the secret reason for his immovability into paternal duty, and it followed by itself that he was justified to call his son's grief stubbornness. In addition, Amadeus's behaviour improved visibly. Soon he was slipping into his clothes, even if it was after the allotted hour.

At last everything seemed to have eaten itself out in his little hard head, and he came along as before, sat opposite his father and watched as per his old, thorough manner as if nothing had happened. And even old Mandel changed with many kindhearted words before his boy. Only he was no longer able to look into the little boy's eyes. For their look was melancholy, as if defeated.

The child sat for hours thus without speaking a word, and observed his father attentively as if a secret lay hidden in him, and when he began to speak, he directed strange questions at the master.

"If a bird falls from a tree, is it dead then?" he once asked.

"Birds don't die", Mandel answered.

"Why don't birds die?"

"Because they have wings and fly away from death."

"But do trees die?" Amadeus asked further.

"Yes, trees die."

"Who lays them in the grave?"

"They don't need a grave. They fall down and remain lying."

After these words of Mandel's, Amadeus went out and looked at the whole world around the tailor's house. When he came back in, he sat himself down away from his father and stared at him ceaselessly for a long time until tears entered his eyes. Then he said quite softly to himself, "Clouds die, the maple dies, the grass and the meadow and everything, everything dies", and did not turn his look away, as if everything stood written in his father sewing there in front of him and not daring to look up.

Thus he strayed with scared soul about a pit within himself.

Sometimes it also went through his mind, 'If I sing, my father will die', and although he did not know what dying was, he took the emptiness and silence to be what flowed out of him into his father's room, lay around the house and filled the whole world, and he thought he was to blame for everything.

Then, to hinder his father from encountering anything so bad, he did everything he could think of:
gathered up the needles, collected them in the little tin
can, layered the little pieces of cloth in a pile, pulled
tacking stitches out of the things and endeavoured to
throw one leg over the other like a proper tailor.

At the same time, he compelled himself to be quiet
and diligent like a beetle. Thus the little boy alone
thought to take away the oppressive and invisibly sinis-
ter thing which was obviously also over his father. And
always, when Amadeus had thus served for hours, he
expected his father to steer his face to him and take pity
on him with many loving words. But each time, the little
fellow was deceived. Only, if Maruschka came in or nodded through the window from without or stepped to the
cutting table and pressed the master's bowed head still
lower with a playful dab, a radiance ran right through
Christoph Eusebius and opened his wrinkled eyes to a
wide glance. Then the boy suffered deeper the feeling
which hurt him so, the way nostalgia pains grown ups.

At such moments of hidden disappointment,
Amadeus did not remain in his father's room anymore,
and the unease which had come to him from Eusebius's
travel stories opened its door to him without him needing to knock. It drove him from the house and was like a
scourge behind him so that he ran faster and ever faster
down the first good summer-dry slope which came under his feet. He was not enticed by that which was close,
but by everything distant, unreachable. Trees on the
furthest horizon, bearing their transparent crowns in
the white March air as if floating, evoked in the child the
wish to stand on the tip of their treetops and see into
the pale expanse of heaven. When men emerged from
the secluded paths, he thought they had appeared because of him and would come, take him affectionately
by the hand and continue with him. He clung with

pounding heart to this conceit until the people became smaller and smaller and finally vanished in the distance. Then Amadeus felt as if a light had been extinguished and he was standing alone again in the invisible darkness.

Even the drainage ditches did it to the boy. He ran with their waves until he could hardly find his way back anymore. When, on his way home, he skimmed past the houses whose windows and doors lay in the light, he felt the urge in himself to step over the strange threshold and ask for lodging.

Little Amadeus was like a bird whose song autumn has destroyed and now must stray anxiously and restlessly through the fields.

When the boy returned to the Mandel house hours later, he was met by his parents very seriously. His father heaped long abusive sermons on him, the mute woman spawned formless, rumbling sounds and gauged him with her brown, uncannily empty eyes.

Over where he had been and what he was after outside, Amadeus did not know what to say. Pale and apprehensive, he pressed himself into a corner and suffered everything with a feeling as if he were sitting in a strange house.

One day little Mandel had served once again in vain for his father's love, and crept over the threshold, not like a child who has his home there, but like one who has begged in vain for alms and now leaves in shame. Then he felt in his trouser pocket, between the laces and little sticks, a crumpled-up ball of paper, and when he unfolded it, there was a number of those little strips on which he had drawn the tracks of songs which had come to him secretly behind his father's back. That meant for Amadeus, to begin with, a happy discovery, and he now knew from where it sometimes flashed around him, distant and melodious. But it also soon occurred to him that it was perhaps the reason why his father had not yet forgiven him. The longer he thought about it, the more dangerous the mute songs he carried around with him seemed to the boy. But he could not manage to part from them and continued to hold them hidden under the laces and pieces of wood in his pocket.

Then the distant, fleeting sounds were thrown out to him more often. The needles which he collected skipped ringing into the little tin, his father's voice did not jar so strangely, his figure no longer looked so painfully crushed and even before Maruschka herself, he felt surer, as if behind a palely lit wall.

This last traffic with his deepest desire lasted, however, only a few days.

He had piled on the cutting table next to his father two little heaps of cloth scraps and was playing with them by seizing a little scrap with each hand and throwing them both from one hand to the other. To start with, he did not have much success with the game, for the scraps seemed to have a mind of their own after the hands had released them, springing next to the chair, under the table or in another place where Amadeus did not want to have them. For that reason, Amadeus reprimanded them for their waywardness, talked to them affectionately too, paid precise attention, and had them after some time so well trained that they found their way easily from his left to his right and flitted playfully by one another. Soon they were not even cloth scraps anymore, but little birds which flew from his hands and returned obediently again and, not long after, they began to sing to each other when they were fluttering.

Suddenly the enraptured child was seized roughly by the arm, and a shrill, angry voice screamed, "Boy, you are surely the devil's!"

Amadeus started from his tossing, the last tone remained stuck in his mouth and he looked into the face of his father. It was pale, his lips were trembling, his breathing was as if he were about to suffocate, and a strand of grey hair hung over his brow.

Then the child thought no less than that his father was passing away. He threw himself across the tailor's knees and begged him not to die, he would truly never do it again.

Then he went furtively out onto the bench outside the house and did not doubt anymore that the mute songs were to blame for everything, and he saw that he would have to part from them if he did not want his father to perish miserably. A fleeting wind was skimming through the twisted willow just then. Without hesitating, Amadeus sought out the paper ball and decided it was best to let the songs fly into the air. He had of course received them from the clouds, the trees and the sun. Then each could seek out the place from which it had come to him.

Hardly had the boy let the first little strip out of his hand than it was seized by the wind and conducted high up into the air. 'Aha', Amadeus thought, that is a song of the sun and wants to go up into the heavens. But it swirled a few times around the roof's gutters and then acted as if it had a desire to climb into the maple. But when it had already got quite close to the lowest branch, it thought of another, fluttered down, swayed around a few times indecisively and then skimmed the extended flight to the window, to whose panes it cleaved. There it remained stuck and immediately raised a cheerful piping with the wind.

Then the child saw that his songs could not be disposed of in this way without endangering his father. For if he just opened the window, the wind would fly into the room with the song and his father would plunge directly from the cutting table into the mortuary.

For that reason, Amadeus caught the little strip again, crumpled it into the ball of paper, stuck it in his pocket, returned to the room and waited for a favourable moment. Then his father nodded to Maruschka and left the room with her. They both went up the stairs to the loft. Its steps still creaked a few times now and then. After that there was silence and Amadeus was alone.

He opened the stove door quickly and threw the ball of paper into the fire. But because he was too agitated, he aimed badly and they did not end up in the middle of the embers, but fell by the edge at the front where a few red coals were spitting from the heat as if they would like most of all to spring out of the box and run away. But hardly had the ball spent a while in their society, quiet and motionless, than it was frightened to death, recovered itself and began to transform. A stretching went through it. From within, a hidden force began to smoulder. With soft crinkling, it folded itself up like a flower over which the magic of blooming has come.

The fire nearby flared with its white radiance, astonished over the transformation of the ball of paper. Then it sprang over twitching to see everything exactly. But as soon as its little flames ran blue and gold over the paper, the songs on them began to sing and trill. Sometimes it even sounded like a high pitched crying, like sobbing and swallowing. A glaring brilliance poured out of the stove box and flowed out along the wall. Amadeus slammed the door shut in fright, so that the brilliance of the songs did not fly into the room, and he ran in fear from the house.

When he ventured in again, his father was sitting as always in the tailor's enclosure, pale and exhausted. His eyes were glowing in powerless, sorrowfull intoxication and looked from time to time at his hands which were folded worn and idle over his work. Maruschka was standing at the cupboard and letting a little sack of peas run into a large clay pot.

The fiery glow of the songs did not illuminate the walls anymore and their quiet voices had been burnt up for ever. The air hung falteringly and grey in the room and the boy was overcome by such a dark, boundless solitude that he crept behind a cupboard and cried silently to himself.

12

Since the day on which Amadeus had incinerated his mute songs, the boy's life drew back more and more from its accustomed mode and fell into the waters of a subterranean current which was bearing him to an unknown outlet. The little boy knew nothing. Nothing but a painful anticipation was in him.

One evening the invisible thing which always rambled about the Mandel house entered the tailor's living room and took the boy with it.

Old Mandel had not completed his day's work. He pulled the piece on which he was working neatly together and shoved it under the bench, gathered together the equipment on the table, spooled the thread on the machine's shuttle, in short, he prepared everything so that the old little wheel could be driven on the next morning without delay. After that he slipped out of his weekday rags and into a better spencer behind the wardrobe door. Several important considerations tumbled about in his face and when he had half ironed them out, he stepped up to Maruschka and pushed her to hurry too with a silent whirl of his hands. — The housekeeper gave this demand a contented smile. She left the room, and the tailor placed himself before the window and looked out into the grey of the evening.

Why has my father put on a different coat? Why does he stand and look out at the world? Why did he send my Maruschka mother out? What does he want to do with me and her? They perhaps won't go away, leave me here, not return anymore, wander in a strange land entirely outside Prussia and buy themselves a new boy?

All that swirled through Amadeus's head as he observed his father with aching bewilderment while he still stood at the window and now began to drum with his long fingernails impatiently on the window sill. At the same time, he lifted his head again and again with gentle sniffs. This constant coming apart of his compressed back brought forth the idea in the child that his father was making a face which he had never seen before. Just as Amadeus wanted to stand up to observe what was happening with his face that made his father snap up and down with his back without stopping, Maruschka entered the room. She placed a little pot on the table and laid a thick slice of bread with it. That was to be the boy's supper. Then she drew the colourful scarf properly across her shoulders and jiggled the tailor softly on the shoulder as a sign of her readiness. Eusebius came out of his deep thought, encompassed the mute woman with a happy glance, laid his hand on her breast and shoved her a little to the side to clear the path to his boy.

He watched with an expectation, together with a trembling, that his father was coming to him, and thought, 'My father is coming to me and will take me with him.' Then he shut his eyes in anticipated enjoyment of a cuddle. But Eusebius stopped two steps in front of him and said he should wait until they returned and meanwhile guard the house. There was something to see about in the houses on the mountain. The supper was on the table and if he were tired, he could go to sleep. "But you must by no means make a light," the tailor concluded his words with this command. "Do you hear, Amadeus, don't do any lighting matches. For then the fire wolf will come and devour you along with the house."

The boy sensed his father's other face in the words and wanted to scream, "Father, stay, don't go away. With that face, you won't find your way home again." But a spasm clenched Amadeus's chest. When he had recovered, the steps of them going away were sounding softer and softer through the twilight. But the boy still saw within himself the pair toddling away. Finally they were also no longer to be seen in his thoughts. Horrified, he sprang up and ran out in front of the house to hurry after them. A grey emptiness spread out all around. In this, Amadeus saw Maruschka and his father indistinctly, far off like they were at the end of the world, being carried away, and then vanishing like birds into the clouds.

The boy could not run that far, it was already in a foreign land. And if he got there, he would not know his father anymore because he had gone away with the strange face that he had forgotten to look at.

Despondent, he returned to the living room and cowered on the floor next to the oven.

It was in that late part of the evening when the light of the day has already become so weak that it now only calls up individual waves which hustle across the earth, and behind them waves of deeper shadows always follow. People then say the Lord is falling to sleep above them and already blinking. Thus the lightening and darkening also flowing through the living room of the tailor Eusebius, and Amadeus believed it was the reflection of people walking past outside.

The boy ventured a little step further towards the window and peered out cautiously. At this moment, the mysterious wandering past stopped and there was nothing outside but the twisted willow in the meadow. It bowed its catkin yellow crown of switches down like a bloated shimmering head, as if it were looking at someone at its feet. Amadeus knew of course that it could be nobody but the little stream which the old tree was looking at, but nevertheless did not venture another step forward in curiosity, and stretched his neck out.

But then he was terrified to the depths of his soul. For someone was sitting under the willow. The person had grey garments on and was looking motionless at the little stream. Hazily pale, an ash grey cloth drawn over the head so that Amadeus could discern neither shoulder nor arms, the person crouched there.

She is waiting for me, the boy thought, and wants to take me with her. Noiselessly he drew back his left foot, which he had put forward in the excitement, so as to huddle again on the old rug next to the stove. But this soft shuffling of his soles on the floor, which the boy himself had not heard, must have been perceived by the mysterious woman under the willow. For a billowing came into her, and before Amadeus could sit down, she rose, stretched, wavered in the air and came floating over the meadow straight to the tailor's house.

The boy did not dare to watch what would happen now and shut his eyes in terror. When he opened them again, a face was looking in the window which was similar to the face of farmer Hübner's wife. It smiled, waved to the boy and disappeared.

Then Amadeus grasped the bread on the table and ran hastily from the house.

In the yard of the farmer Schnallke, the gate had just been closed with much banging. A motherly voice was calling from a house in the darkness. The Hainwald forest stood dark and motionless. On the main road, someone was walking with loud steps. Amadeus quickly bit a large chunk from the bread, then placed the slice on a fence post and began to run down the little path through the meadow. The twisted willow reached for him with its switches, but he paid no attention to it. The invisible people whose distant passing-by he had observed from his father's room were around him and, wedged into a current rushing irresistably forward, he was carried onward. Without knowing what was happening to him, he ran along the path to the Röhrsdorf farmsteads. The little knocking man was standing before the bushes of the bump and waved to him. Then the white, flying dress of a little girl scurried through the branches and vanished into the narrow pass. Amadeus spat out the bite that he still had in his mouth, clenched his teeth and began to run forward as fast as he had ever gone in his life before, so that he did not have to go alone through the horrid night of the narrow pass. He tripped, got up, stumbled here and there against the edges. His heart was pounding to bursting.

Finally he stood on the edge of the bush.

The white farmsteads of Röhrsdorf swam uncertainly through the darkness of the basin below him. Amadeus looked for the farmstead of the farmer Hübner, and when he thought he had found it, he shouted shrilly in distressed joy, "Veronika!" and plunged onwards at a hurried run. And while he ran, he spoke constantly to himself, crying and laughing at the same time, "Veronika, I am coming to you. Veronika, I am coming to you … Veronika, I am coming …"

Thus he arrived not long afterwards at the pond which lay not far from the Hübner farmstead among the bushes.

It was quite still and was sleeping blankly and dark. It did not even absorb the shadows of the trees which stood on its banks. Amadeus looked at the water for a long time as it rested there so motionless and mysterious.

The great silence which ran out from it made the tailor's boy despondent so that he did not dare go into the farmyard which looked out at him from between the trees of the garden with two large window-eyes. Their brightness reached out a fair way into the shadowy half darkness and went directly towards the boy.

For that reason, Amadeus thought that if he sat on the grass and waited, Veronika would have to see him with the light from the window, come out to him and fetch him. The night was warm. He crouched in the young grass and began to pluck their narrow leaves and throw them in the pond. But the girl did not want to be seen. Sometimes it seemed to the boy as if she were fumbling her way to him on soft feet, then he said his friend's name happily and looked down at his hands.

But he was always mistaken, and nothing more rang out again but the stamping of the cows and horses from the closed stalls. Yes, when he turned around, the light in the windows was already extinguished and the farmstead lay dark and alien in the falteringly still night. Amadeus could not comprehend why the wife of the farmer Hübner had waved to him from the window, if she had now gone to sleep without fetching him in. He raised his eyes and looked around to consider what to do now. The long bush was leaning straight in front of him like a giant black wall in the sky and behind it, a brightness was swelling up as if someone was passing there with a light.

Then it occurred to the boy that he could wait to see who would climb up there.

It could be someone who would shine on him so that he would not have to sit so lonesomely anymore by the pond which slept without end and paid no attention to him at all. — Slowly the glow went higher, hanging at first little golden nuts here and there in the darkness of the bush, soon after it was stabbing with shimmering wands through the branches, then filling the high vaulted windows of the forest with its radiance, now the black crossed flowers of the highest tips of the spruces emerged in dazzling seething and stood as the round gate in the open sky which the angel with the golden branches had drilled through the blue night.

At the sight of the moon, every fear faded from the poor tailor's boy, for he had seen how in the night of his earliest childhood, a gleaming road had flowed from the round gate of the moon and streamed down over the forest. The figure of his heavenly mother, which he had longed for at the time, arose in him and now he also knew that it had not been the farmer Hübner's wife, but she who had waved to him through the window.

The shackles of the enforced silence fell from Amadeus's soul. The play of soft wings flittered to him and at once he heard again from the bright depths within himself the sound of the music of the golden branches with which angels lure men from the earth. The submerged jubilation of his songs awoke in him. He rose to sing the streams of light, the darkness of the long bush, the song of the nocturnal blue sky, his loneliness, and his longing that someone would caress him and fondly take his little hands.

He noticed that his heavenly mother was listening to him, for her silvery path was flowing ever closer to him and was already gliding from the opposite shore into the pond, which awoke thereby and began to tremble restively with thousands of ripples.

Suddenly Amadeus heard his name called through the song.

It sounded distant and anxious, "Amadeus! — Amadeus!!"

The boy fell silent in dismay. For he thought his mother was calling him, and yet it also seemed to him that the voice was coming from another direction.

He stood up and looked around, but saw nothing except a large grey bird flying just then over the slopes of Upper Röhrsdorf through the countryside. It was flying very awkwardly. Amadeus noticed how it was always pushing itself off from the ground with its legs and then fluttering with short wings for a stretch. Once more the call seemed to come weakly from the surrounding area. Then the bird vanished behind a low rise.

The boy turned to the pond again. — The silvery road had meanwhile moved halfway across the pond. Amadeus saw that he must wait until it had swum over to him. Then he wanted to let himself down over the edge and go hurriedly to his mother.

Already the branches of the bushes were shimmering over him in white brilliance. The waves rocked the path ever closer. The grass at his feet began to glimmer. Now the shining road was at the bank.

Amadeus was seized by delight and ardency.

Smiling and affectionate, he whispered, "My dear mother. My dear mother."

At the same time, he let himself slowly glide down over the bank.

But before his feet touched the glittering stones, it wheezed up to him from behind, whistling.

He was grasped by the armpits and ripped out of his intoxication.

When he turned around, he looked into the contorted face of his father, who drew him close and immediately began to cry.

After the tailor Mandel had calmed down somewhat, he asked his boy, "But, Amadeus, tell me just, what were you wanting to do?"

The boy extracted himself from his father's embrace and said coolly and soberly, "I wanted to go to my mother."

And after a hesitation, he added, sadly and reproachfully, "Then you came."

Then he fell silent, lowered his head and was led home.

13

After the tailor Mandel had such a night whistle around his ears, it was no longer necessary for him to look for stones on which he had to step.

Incidentally, it became as easy for Christoph Eusebius as all things become to us which can be thus and no different.

When he stepped out of his house in the morning and saw the maple spreading its crown over the roof in a way as if they were not branches and twigs with thickly swollen buds, but giant wings dotted green and swaying playfully so that you could think it would fly away any moment, the tailor said to himself in the silence, "It certainly will do that."

And everywhere had meanwhile turned to sunlight. Sunlight, not perhaps such as the winter trapped with irritated hand and crushed and crumbled before it let it out, no, a light lay over Upper Röhrsdorf which came and immediately shone over all the mountains. Over the long bush where it had come from, thought Eusebius.

Yes and actually on no day of his life had the houses and little farms of his native place seemed like a herd of colourful cattle who were romping about in a muddle on the rolling plain and pushing together narrowly there where the plateau climbed up to the distant forest, as if each wanted to vanish first into the dark green and go away over the border to Bohemia.

"For ever, of course", Eusebius said. There must and should never be any going back.

In such an entangled way, the tailor gathered his intentions from the world around him. Then he went into the living room, sought out Amadeus's slate from its hiding place and wrote his intentions on it. It was before people were about that he did all that. The smoke had yet to awake in any of the chimneys all around. The Lord alone was walking across the fields and talking with soft breath to his trees, and little Amadeus lay and slept as if the angel were carrying him in a shimmering net across the earth.

After Mandel had come to an end with his writing task, he sat down at the cutting table and waited with his hands jammed between his knees. Finally he heard Maruschka get up and come down the loft stairs. Then he turned pale all over, picked up the slate, went towards the woman and handed to her what he had written. He stood so upright like he had never stood opposite a person in his life, not even Napoleon himself; but he could not look at Maruschka. He placed himself by the window and looked out.

A trembling minute passed. Then he heard the tablet being put down and the housekeeper stepping back.

So, thank God, now it's over, Mandel thought, and waited a little while so that the mute woman could go away. But when he turned around, she was standing there and staring with wide eyes into a pot which she had absentmindedly taken from the cupboard. The tears were running over her cheeks so that one caught the other.

Resolutely he stepped up to her. But it did not last long before she had recovered. Finally she lifted her head like an over-heavy weight and looked questioningly at the sleeping child. Eusebius nodded, and because the mute woman still could not resign herself to the irrevocable, he wrote with shaking arms in the air that she had to leave instantly. He, Eusebius Mandel, and the King of Prussia no longer wanted it.

After that he turned around and sat on his bed with face averted.

The door shut.

The stairs creaked.

Then a chest was being dragged in the chamber above him. After that something large, soft fell over.

'Now she has collapsed in a faint', the tailor thought.

And suddenly it became silent in the house, so deathly still that Mandel could not bear it.

He sank down and covered his face with the bedcovers. He remained lying there thus until Maruschka had left the house.

When he stepped to the window again, he saw the mute woman with a large pack on her back, bent forward, but walking with long, steady strides along the stony path to the houses on the mountain. Something like a darkening in the high heavens ran with her wherever the woman turned in her path, as if her body were not throwing its shadow next to her but up into the air. Hardly had Christoph Eusebius seen that, than he knew what that meant, fetched the slate on which he had written his last words to Maruschka and the pot in which her tears had fallen, carried them into the Hainwald forest to an isolated spot, smashed them on a stone, and buried the shards in the ground.

Then he returned to his house and opened the chest in which he had stored the clothes of his dead wife Agathe, took out a jacket, a skirt and underskirt, a bodice, and all that belonged to a woman's attire. He hung it all on the hooks next to Amadeus's bed as if his Agathe had never died, but just gone away for a time and could return any moment. — Meanwhile his sleeping boy stirred towards waking.

Mandel stepped to the bed, stroked the pale blond hair gently from his forehead and woke him fully with a kiss, "Good morning, Amadeus," he said, "just look, the sun has already been awake a long time, and I think the birds are also singing already."

And in the afternoon, the tailor sat in his enclosure and worked. From time to time, his glance lifted and skimmed over the meadow to the Hainwald forest. It was now completely unwed to winter and fully awake. The blue grandeur of its depths streamed ceaselessly from it and breathed at first as a scented shadow of the sun across the young green of the meadow. But then it weaved itself into the light, stood as a trembling shimmer over its sharp treetops and reached over even as far as Eusebius's chest, in which a dark, silent, aching feeling still lay in its last convulsions. For a long while, this indescribable breath of the forest fumbled about at the jammed, bony door of the tailor's chest without entering. But in the end, the many shunted bolts gave way and Eusebius Mandel had a feeling as if his heart would be taken in gentle hands and unfolded like a flower.

The feeling was so exceptionally precious that the tailor looked around astonished, as if it were possible to perceive that being from which this magical blessing had issued. And really, Christoph Eusebius's eyes had not been searching for a long time in wondering expectation over the thousand blue shadow gates of the Hainwald forest, when he saw his Agathe emerge out of the darkness, just as she had been in life, and now knew who had turned his inner being all of a sudden thus towards grace. But now his wife's head was not bowed like the other time when he had seen her for the first time since her death. She bore her narrow, calm face uplifted. The colourful ribbons of her bonnet played around her forehead and she held her prayer book with gentle hand pressed to her breast and the wide pleated skirt stirred with her steady gait. The most light, however, welled from her face.

When she had gotten as far as the edge of the shadow with which the forest was reaching out into the meadow, she faded away. Only the shimmer of her eyes remained in the air and wafted on a straight path towards his house as if she were wandering through her gaze from the other side into the tailor's place under the maple, where she had lived so long as a person.

The Röhrsdorf tailor saw a white light coming through the window to him in his little room and when he dared to turn around, he saw how his dead wife floated back and forth as a bright radiance on the floor.

Just then he wanted to tell his boy, "Look, that is your heavenly mother," but it was not necessary. Little Amadeus was sitting on the chair next to the pot cupboard and following with his eyes the play which the reflection of the white clouds was making in the tailor's room.

For that reason, Eusebius made no sound, turned around again soundlessly and waited for what his boy would say about it himself.

It lasted not three seconds, then the little boy began, not to speak, but to sing. At first it rang softly like the song of the robin which in the darkness of the bush dithers to itself. But then it lengthened out further and further into the free and happy, and assisted the tailor's house and everyone in it back to their earlier wondrous souls. That is why the tailor did not need at first to ask Amadeus whether he knew who had come to visit them. It sounded from every corner; old, blessed raptures awoke in the rough walls. The twisted willow was moved so that the golden dust of its catkins flew around its crown of switches like a halo, and Eusebius was so occupied by it that he doubled the yarn and saw his world again in thousandfold colourfulness.

About the Publisher

Our mission is to provide translations into English of the complete works of neglected major European writers. We do not cherry-pick works that seem the most marketable, but rather seek to provide a complete collection of each writer's works so that readers can follow the writer's development and decide on its merits for themselves.

http://www.facebook.com/KANitzPublishing